LIVING HAUNTED

LIZZY RICHMOND

LIVING HAUNTED

BOOK TWO

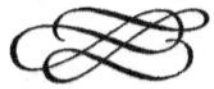

LIZZY RICHMOND

First paperback edition October 2023

Book design by MiblArt

Edited by April Kelly

ISBN 979-8-9870771-1-5 (paperback)

ISBN 979-8-9870771-2-2 (ebook)

www.lizzyrichmondsbook.com

❀ Created with Vellum

*To my Aunt Lydia for being my personal cheerleader.
I love you!*

PROLOGUE

"Long ago, before kingdoms divided themselves under different rulers, certain Gods would walk amongst their people. The ogres and the giants, the witches and the fairies, the humans and the elves—they were all united by the Gods they both loved and feared.

Then a war came and changed everything. Not a war on Earth, but a war among the Gods. Before this war, they were able to control who came down to interact with the people on Earth. It's what kept anyone from disobeying them. Gods were kind to those who loved them and punished those who became a problem.

After the war, no one could control what Gods came down to Earth. The corruption spread like wildfire. Killings, wars, division of property arose. Kings and Queens were crowned rulers, and the Gods gained less and less of their devotion.

It was said there was only one God that looked down at the changes with sadness. They could no longer stop what was happening. The God knew they must repair their own home before trying to fix the world underneath.

One night, under the full moon, a drunken merchant made it home to his wife and two children. His wife had begged him to stop drinking, but knowing there was no hope, she started to hide some of the gold he would bring home. Not enough that he would notice, but enough to slowly build a way to take her children to safety. The drunk merchant wanted nothing to do with his eldest daughter, who was only five years of age, and less of his son, only one week old.

No one knows what was said. Only that when the moon hit its apex, the man held his newborn son in his hand, making his way to a clearing deep in the woods. Everyone knew not to travel in the woods at night, but somehow, the man got in and out without a single scratch. The same couldn't be said about the baby.

When morning came and the woman noticed her infant son to be missing, she went looking for him. She and her daughter ran through the woods in search of the baby, even though the woman knew no infant could survive a night in the woods alone. She didn't care. Something drove her to look no matter how long it took.

When she found the baby, he wasn't crying. He was laughing. Basking in the sunlight. All alone. The woman knew the baby was her son, but when she had seen the golden shine coming from his eyes, her breath caught in her throat. She had known what it meant.

He was chosen by the Gods. He was destined to do great things. Things his father could never dream of.

And he did.

He grew up with a purpose. He was able to travel through the shadows of the night, righting wrongs and punishing the victimizers. He had his purpose and for half of his life, that was enough for him. Until the day a snake whispered in his ear. He was as great as the Gods. He had the power to rule.

He was stronger than all the armies and crowns of reigning kingdoms. He **deserved** to rule everything.

What he didn't see was the Gods that watched him from the skies. They knew he was being driven by his greed. Some say they gave him chances to come back to them. Gave him chances to do what was right, but alas, he did what anyone drunk on power and greed would do. He went further and further into the darkness until the Gods were left with no choice but to stop him.

So, that is what they did.

They went to the one person who had been devoted to them since she saw what their grace could do to someone at only five years of age. She prayed every morning and every night. She spent her days trying to spread the kindness of the Gods. Her heart was pure and her mind untainted. That night they sent a messenger God to travel to her dreams. They told her she must right the wrong taking over her family.

No matter how crushed she was to take down someone she loved for someone else she loved, she did it. All her powers were given to her by the Gods and with her last breath, she created a veil trapping in every truly horrid thing...including her own brother."

He stood in the darkened corner of the room, his hands forming a fist as he listened to her story. He debated crushing her throat the second she started, but he needed her alive. His golden eyes looked up at Anna with no signs of the anger deep in his soul. "I'm sure there is a point you are trying to make with this story," he stated.

She looked up from the glass of tea in her hand. A small smile spreading on her face, "If you used to be a God, what are you now?"

CHAPTER 1

Four weeks. Three days. Four hours. 36 minutes. 37, 38, 39 seconds. That's how long it had been since the war that took everything I didn't realize I wanted… or needed. I knew I shouldn't have been counting. Every second I knew would pass made me unable to focus on anything else. Every lesson I had to go through, every meditation, and every meeting went to the back of my mind. All I could think about was how I failed. I was supposed to save everyone and too many of them died. Kit died.

I SAT in the center of my bedroom, dressed in a red robe flowing around me. My legs were crossed, and I rested the backside of my palms on my knees. I focused on my breathing hoping to quell the moving fire that circled inside of me. Beginning to learn even a fraction of my powers was beyond difficult. I spent every day trying different medicines, different calming techniques, and for the first couple of weeks, everyone just left me angry.

Well, all but one.

One made me depressed. I sobbed until there were no tears left. I stayed in my bed so long people had to check on me to make sure I was still alive. Then I made a mistake… well, a sort of mistake. I thought it was a mistake when I did it, but now I knew it was probably the only way I was able to make it through that night.

I didn't know how late it was when another person knocked on the door. I didn't care. I couldn't care. I just stayed lying in my bed, swallowed by my mistakes. I saw a small light travel into the room. The light slowly moved into view, and I could see Grace holding a candle in her hand. "I needed to make sure you were still alive in here," she tried to joke, but even the small smile on her face showed nothing but worry. It seemed to be second nature to her, but there was something different with her worry now than when we first met. This wasn't a worry that came about with trying to return life to the way it was supposed to be. It was a broken worry. The worry you hold after you've lost so much because you don't think you could take any more.

She turned around, about to walk away, when I heard words that didn't sound like they came from me, but they did. "I don't want to be."

She stopped, turning around to look at me. If she had anything to do for the next twenty-four hours, she didn't show it. Because she didn't leave my side.

AFTER THAT, it only took two failed potions Tasar had made himself, before he was able to find one that worked. I didn't know who Tasar had lost, but I felt like he could understand what I was going through. He didn't treat me like I was falling apart, but every time the wave of reality came over me, he gave me an excuse. A way to avoid falling apart in front of other people. To avoid the looks of pity. I hated the looks of pity.

Once mediation time was over, Mary-Anne and Florence would help me get dressed for the day. They helped me with everyday things I needed done. Florence was open and talkative to the point she would hardly breathe. She was always moving about so fast, that the braid she always had her blonde hair would slowly come apart throughout the day. Mary-Anne was the opposite. She was quiet, and every move she made was calculated. She was terrified the first time she met me, maybe she still was, but at least she looked at me now.

When it came to getting dressed for the day, I didn't argue, I didn't fight what was expected of me. I went into whatever dress was picked out for me. Whether my hair was up or down, I let them make the choice depending on the neckline. There was only one thing I could never get myself to agree to. The idea of wearing a tiara. I couldn't do it. I just couldn't.

I would sit in front of the mirror, my long, soft hair laying in waves over my tense shoulders, and I would remain in contact with the green eyes in front of me. I would find myself staring at the red flecks that danced with the green like they were moving. The second the tiara came close to my head the red in my eyes would intensify. "No!" I would demand and there were no questions, suggestions, or anything else. I was a princess. I didn't have to explain myself to anyone.

The castle wasn't completely put back together after the war and neither were some of the villages, but we were starting to make progress. Many of our soldiers died in the war, and the hundreds of casualties that didn't die from Anna's spell died from illnesses we couldn't cure because we didn't understand them. The only thing that made it easier was focusing on the normality we were trying to get back to.

AFTER GETTING DRESSED, I would walk down the nearly empty halls to whatever class or meeting I was supposed to attend and the only sound I could really hear was my shoes against the marble floor. My mind would get wrapped in the entrancing sound of my steps and my memories took that as an opportunity to twist the knife in my heart.

"I-I-I…" He took a deep breath in, fighting for his words. "I-I love you." I heard one final breath leave his lips.

Those words haunted me. Those words reminded me of his death and my chance at happiness that evaporated in seconds. He wasn't supposed to be there. He was supposed to leave with his brother, but he insisted. I wish I would have said something. I wish I had fought for him to leave. We wouldn't have been together, but he would be alive. I would give anything to go back to that. To change it, but I can't.

The only thing I could do was to be better. Get better. Get more control. Nothing could be taken from me if I knew how to control my powers. So, that's what I did. I focused on all the books, all the papers, all the maps, all the charts. I was doing better than most had expected. Most expected me to break.

Grace made sure to hire a tutor in order to avoid any arguments like we had in the beginning. His name was Professor Aaron Barter. He was the same height as me, double my age, with a full head of black hair, dark brown eyes that almost looked black, and a baby face—which I will admit made it hard to listen to him at first.

He would be going through the different kingdoms surrounding Neville and all I could do was stare at him. He would try his hardest to ignore the fact he knew I wasn't listening. Professor Barter would just sigh, angrily putting his hands on his hips, until finally he would tilt his head, "Princess, are you going to actually listen or am I wasting my time?" he asked, and I felt my head tilt as well.

"I just don't understand."

This made him soften, "What do you need help with?"

"How someone can be the age of…forty-four and still look so young?"

Professor Barter huffed, plopping down on the chair next to me. "Do you know why I took this job?"

"Because the Queen asked you and who says no to royalty?"

"Because I know there is no way you would be able to learn all of this with some random tutor. Yes, they could be good at their job, but you are lacking the required education you should have gotten as a child. You needed someone who was going to be able to apply the childhood lessons in a way your grownup self can process and evolve in a shorter period. Hopefully, before you are coronated."

I paused, staring at him only for a moment. "Are you calling me dumb?" I asked and he sighed again.

"I'm stating, if a child can learn who is the neighbor to Neville's north, so should a Princess of twenty and two." Professor Barter stood up from the table, looking back at the map he had hanging on a board.

"Muria," I answered, getting him to look back at me. "Just because your being as whole fascinates me, doesn't mean I wasn't listening."

MORNINGS WERE THE EASY PART. It was when nighttime came around, and the pit of emptiness inside of me couldn't be as easily ignored. After dinner, I would walk towards the garden on the castle grounds. Tobyn, Kit's older brother, didn't have much to say after I told him about his brother. No, he had a lot to say about me, but as to what to do with Kit's body, all he knew was Kit wanted to be burned. 'He didn't want to be kept,' as Tobyn was so kind as to put it. He was a mess the first time I met him, from all the drinking and whatever else he got himself into. I destroyed his life the second I went missing on his watch, and I destroyed his life when I took his brother away from him.

I understood why he was so upset, and I had to accept that I couldn't make it better. He didn't like me when Kit was alive. He certainly wasn't going to like me after I got him killed. So, that only left me to have Kit's body cremated and put his remains in the garden. I'm not sure if the garden would have been his choice, but he never said what would have. I never thought to ask.

I would sit on the bench, crossing my legs under my dress so it would hang around me. Then I would just watch the flowers. I think a part of me was wondering if the wind was strong enough and I was listening hard enough, maybe I could hear his voice again. A part of me told myself it was a hope that would never be true, but I still hoped. Day after day, night after night.

No one bothered me when I was out here. They seemed to know better. At first, Abbey, the woman who would have been my nanny, would try to get me inside to get ready for bed, but after my demand that she get the hell away from me and not bother me again, there was never another problem. I know she meant well. Every time I was with her, it was clear she wanted to take care of me. Knowing that didn't change the fact I didn't want to see people. I didn't need to. Sometimes, especially when it was dark enough that the stars started to shine, Axel would come out of the woods and sit with me. It was the only time I was able to see him. He was just a big wolf, but when I was around him, I felt safer. He was another part of Kit that I was able to hold onto.

Axel would get up and head into the woods before I would go into the castle. I felt like I didn't have the right to leave him. I was the reason he was spending his days alone. Once inside, I would go to my bedroom, let Florence and Mary-Anne get me ready for bed, and then I would dismiss them. They had no reason to believe I wouldn't be going to bed. I never did, but they didn't need to know that. They only needed to know what I told them.

They didn't need to know that I waited until the castle was completely silent to leave my room. Until there was only the light from the moon and the candle in my hand before I would leave my bedroom again. The marble was cold against my bare feet, but I happened to like it. The castle was never so cold that the long nightgown I was in couldn't keep me warm. I would go down the hall to the side stairs that traveled all the way up one of the towers. On the top floor of the tower was only one room. Since I started spending so much time in it, I needed a reason to be there. If I spent all my time in an empty, dusty room, everyone would question it and I would be forced to let others in. So, I went with the first thing I came up with. The light and view from the only window, and the silence away from everyone else, made it the perfect place for an art studio.

I was never that good at art. I would never be put in museums, but I knew enough to make paintings Grace seemed to enjoy. Every now and then I would give her one to hang up, with the promise she wouldn't put it in a common area, and she got me everything she thought I would need. Things I didn't ask for, or even think to ask for.

Once I was inside the now-lively art studio, I would make sure the door was shut and locked. During the day, I would even place a chair against it to make sure no one could come in without me knowing.

I walked towards the wall across from the single window, lifting my hand to feel a warm red glow surround my hand and move to the tips of my fingers. I moved it over the placement of the door, watching it appear. The door was black with gold snakes running along the edges.

The second my hand touched the cold handle, anger rushed over me. I hated to see her, but I had no other choice. I stepped into the room to see Anna standing by the fireplace in a loose-fitting black dress. She was still as thin as before, her hair just as long and black, but her eyes were less black, more brown. She had more life in death than she ever had before. It made me hate her even more.

"You took longer this time to show," Anna said, tossing pages of one of her books in the fire as she ripped them out.

"I am not bringing you more books," I stated, shutting the door behind me and leaning against it. It was the best way to ensure I could keep the most distance from her.

"I believe you said that you wouldn't bring me food as well."

I could sense her smirk without even having to see it. "If I let you die, I lose the chance to fix what you broke!" I snapped.

"I broke?" Anna turned around to look at me as she tossed the final page into the fire. "Pretty sure I didn't kill myself."

"You said you would tell me what I needed. I've played your games for long enough. I'm tired of the riddles and the stories. Tell me what I want to know, or you die in here."

"You'll kill me? And let your poor hunter turn into dust? Well, stay as dust, I guess."

I could feel the rage inside of me starting to boil. My hands itched to hurt her. Maybe not kill her, but to make her suffer. "I will leave you up here and if I don't visit you, you will die in here. No knows you're here. Even if they did, I doubt anyone would care. You are here to give me what I want, and I will not ask again."

Anna paused for a moment, staring at me. She still had that stupid smirk on her face. All she did was chuckle slightly as she walked over to the cushioned red chair in the room. "You've got more fire in you than before. I respect that. It's going to be the end of you, but that's no concern of mine."

I only rolled my eyes, waiting for her to continue.

"There's a book—well, a journal, but it's not as if someone is still writing in it. It's supposed to be preserved in the library. Before you were born, some nobody was able to create a way for it to be preserved without being stuck in a special case. Now, it's used as a history lesson for the kids when they take their yearly tour of the castle."

"What is in the journal?"

"It's the journal of the one who created the veil. It will have the spell and ingredients you will need."

Instead of staying in the room with someone that I hated to look at, I pushed myself off the doorway, about to leave, when she called my name.

"I'm warning you. You might not want to go through with this. It's not going to be as simple as you think."

"I think taking advice from you is the last thing I would do," I stated without a single glance before walking out the door. She was useful for one thing and the second she stopped being useful…well, it's not like anyone would be able to find her.

CHAPTER 2

round lunch time, I had fully intended to spend my time in the library looking for the book, but Grace sent word asking for me to join her for tea. I wasn't going to say no to her. I couldn't do that to her—no, I could—but I didn't want to answer questions that came with telling her no. I noticed that rather quickly.

I walked into her tearoom made of light colors: whites, creams, light blues, light pinks. It was a large room for the one person sitting on the white couch in the center of the room. Even with the noise of my shoes on the marble floor, Grace hadn't noticed I entered the room. Her couch faced the wall of windows and French doors that led to the balcony on the other side. They were open, letting in the light breeze that moved the soft, blush-colored curtains. "Grace?" I asked, making her jump slightly. "I didn't mean to scare you." I took a seat on the powder-blue chair next to the couch.

Grace snorted, shaking her head, "Don't be silly. You didn't frighten me. I was just lost in my own head." She stood up walking towards the tea tray she kept off to the side away from the couch. "Milk and sugar, correct?"

I nodded even though she wasn't looking at me. She didn't need my answer. She asked every time. I think it was just in case I changed my mind. I didn't. I didn't know what kind of tea she had people making for her, but it needed all the help it could get. I would ask, but I noticed she took her tea very seriously.

"There's a lot to think about when you are planning a coronation," Grace turned around with my cup of tea in her hands.

Alas, the coronation I didn't want. "I still don't know why we need one," I stated, taking the tea from her.

Grace smiled at me softly before walking over to grab her cup off the coffee table and over towards the tray to warm it up, "Every prince or princess has one. It's when other royals can come together in the joy of a party to celebrate and show their support for you."

"Somehow, I don't think they support me." I tried to mutter that under my breath, but seeing Grace snap her head towards me showed me that I failed.

"Why would you say such a thing?"

I sighed, "Grace, I know you are trying to protect my feelings, but news, especially gossip, travels through this castle faster than the cold that moved through the servants last week."

No one knows who started it, but there were many accusations. I'm pretty sure it was Florence, but I'm not going to call her out like that. Either way, it got so bad we had to quarantine them away from the rest of us until they felt better. Watching people go from having servants do everything to going one day without them, I thought the castle was going to burn down. Mary-Anne was the only one that didn't get sick. To keep her from being overrun by the entire castle, every hour I would force her to help me with something to give her a little breathing time. I think that was when she decided to stop being so scared of me.

I remember when I first met her, and she refused to look up at me. When she did, she would look away from me the second she thought I might be looking back at her. I couldn't blame her. As far as she was concerned, I was going to be the end to everything she knew…darkness, destruction, and death.

I quickly shook my head, and the destructive thoughts filling it were quickly pushed aside, "Plus, there is at least one person that doesn't feel the need to spare my feelings."

"Who? I will handle it."

Defeat flashed over me as I reached over to set my teacup on the table next to me, "I don't want you to spare my feelings. I want to know these things. I have a lot to work on and blindly walking around isn't going to help anyone."

Grace sighed, walking back over to her spot, and sitting back down, "I guess I can see your point. I do think there is a way to ease people's worries."

"And how do we do that?"

"I know a big part of people's worries surround how long you spent away from your home and the number of customs that you may not know yet."

I could sense she was building up to something, and I just knew I didn't want to know what it was.

"They might feel better if they knew you were to be…wed shortly after your coronation."

Her words seemed to come out in a different language. I just sat there staring at her with nothing but confusion. My brain refused to process what she was trying to tell me.

"Maisey?"

"I don't…I don't understand what you are trying to tell me."

"I think it would ease everyone's worries if you had plans

to marry after you become Queen and that you had someone lined up."

That time I understood, and my body started to heat with instant rage, "I don't need some man to come save me." Kit saved you. I cursed myself at even pointing the thought out to myself. "It's one thing to think I can't do this because, hell, I'm not sure I can do this, but to suggest everyone would be better off with some random man being in charge... I can't believe you would even suggest such a thing!" I didn't realize I had stood from my chair. "I will not marry some random man!"

"Maisey—"

"I have things to do!" I snapped before storming out of the room. I made it halfway back towards the library when I lost all the steam I had before. Everyone thinks you can't do this...Everyone knows you are a failure. Maybe they're right. Maybe I can't. It's not like I stayed because I had this big dream.

"Please tell me you aren't sick." I looked up to see Tasar standing in front of me, the inside of his elbow covering his nose and mouth.

"Why do you think I'm sick?"

He slowly moved his elbow down, circling his face with his finger to indicate my own, "You look a little pale."

"No, that's just my skin," I remarked, letting out a deep breath. "Grace thinks I need to get married to settle everyone's nerves." I walked past him and Tasar turned on his heel to walk next to me.

"It's not that much of a surprise."

"Are you telling me that you don't think I can do this alone?" You don't even plan on doing this alone. I had to learn to shut off that voice in my head.

"I'm saying that this is how things are done. I mean, King Lucious was engaged when he was seven. Mind you, things changed between then and when he married Queen Grace, but everyone knew he was going to be married shortly after the coronation. He would have been married sooner if a war hadn't broken out."

"So, everyone wants it because it's tradition?"

"No, I'm saying your mother wants it for tradition. Everyone else doesn't think you can handle it."

I scoffed, laughing for the first time in so long.

"People don't usually find me that funny," he mumbled.

"That's because you're not, but you're honest, and I appreciate it." I patted Tasar on the shoulder before walking away in the direction of the library.

I tried to look for the book on my own. The little black signs put up for the kids' tours stayed up and I thought I could just follow them, but every stop that I made failed to give me what I wanted. I felt like I was moving in a circle. Then I realized I was moving in a circle, because the tour was quite literally a circle around the library. It took everything I had not to scream when I realized that. The book isn't here! There is no way that the book is here! I'm going to kill Anna! Yup, it's time for her to die!

I stormed back out of the library heading towards the back staircase. No one was there when I made it through the door leading towards the staircase. There were no noises as I made it up the stairs. Then I heard it. The sound of a door shutting at the top of the stairs. I held up the bottom of my dress, quickening my pace. I made towards the top of the staircase just as Jedediah was about to step down. The first time I met Jedediah, he only had blonde stubble on his chin with a balding head, but his grief hadn't been kind to him or his beer belly.

I stopped, letting my dress fall back down as I glared up at him. "What do you think you're doing?" I asked, not hiding the anger in my voice.

"You spend a lot of time here. It's my job to make sure it's secure."

"You think I'm going to be attacked by some paint and brushes?" I felt my head give a patronizing tilt.

"I was just doing my job."

"I know exactly what you are doing," I stepped closer, invading his space of safety as I joined him on the top step. "And if I see you snooping again, you won't just lose your job." I felt my vision slowly turn red, waiting for his short nod of understanding before I walked away. I went into the room, slamming the door behind me. My eyes cooled and I walked over to the small window. This was one of the highest vantage points of the castle, making everything else so small down below. My brain fluttered down to how I felt stuck in this world. Stuck around things I never believed could be real. At least before, I was so used to being alone, I didn't care if I stayed that way. Sometimes I envy that Maisey.

The Maisey that believed she was destined to die alone, and there was nothing she could do about it. The powerless Maisey that avoided learning about the past she didn't know for 22 years. The Maisey that didn't have to care about anyone else because she had no one else. The Maisey before Kit.

I stepped away from the window and walked over to the other side of the room. I made the door appear, stepping side. Anna was exactly where I left her. Sitting in her stupid chair. "I didn't find the book!" I snapped at her.

"Maybe you didn't look hard enough. I heard that can be a problem with children."

"First of all, I'm not five. Second of all, it wasn't there!"

Anna paused for a moment, looking up at me with confusion. "And?"

"And? What do you mean, and? Where is it?"

My blood boiled as her laughter hit my ears and I clenched my hands into fists. "You expect me to know where it is? If you haven't noticed, I don't leave this room."

I pressed my lips together, taking a deep breath in and letting it out. "How am I supposed to find the book?" I asked through clenched teeth.

"People are in and out of this castle all the time. Any one of them could have checked it out now that it's easily preserved outside of the case. Did you ask?"

"And what would I say is the reason I need to know?"

"Nothing," Anna scoffed. "You really don't know what fear is, do you?"

"You wanna find out?"

"Don't get all emotional. I'm sure there is someone we both happen to know that is probably keeping a sharp eye on that book you want so bad."

Without another word, I turned on my heel, walking out of the room and taking the door away behind me. I walked over to the nearest table, leaning my hands against it. I was just going to have to wait. I couldn't do anything until the moon rose.

I LOST track of how long I truly waited for him to show up. It wasn't too hard because most of my time now blends. Barely sleeping can do that to you. I was sitting just under the window, pulling my knees to my chest and resting my arms on them. "Sorry to keep you waiting." I looked up to see him peering down at me with his gold-flecked eyes, dressed in his usual black button-up, black dress pants, but missing his gold cloak he carried over his shoulders.

"Dressing down, Odes?" I asked, pushing myself up from the ground.

"Who am I to keep a princess waiting?" A smirk peeked from his lips, and I crossed my arms.

"I need a book."

He nodded, looking away from me as he walked around the room, "The journal of Lady Ophelia."

"I don't know where it is."

"Last I heard one of her Gods freaks had it," Odes stopped, staring at the painting in front of him. "This is rather dark."

"It's just the black background," I stated, and he nodded. "Now, 'Gods freaks' is rather harsh, but I'm assuming you mean a priest."

"Same thing." He turned around, looking over at me. "You find him, and you'll get the book."

I crossed my arms, trying not to roll my eyes as well. "I'm sure there is more than one priest in Neville."

He looked at me, putting his hands in his pockets, "I think you know someone who can lead you straight to them."

A breeze of wind blew into the room, and he was gone with it. I groaned, throwing my hair back. He's the most unhelpful person I have ever met! Yet, he's not wrong. There's only one person that I know has a strong relationship with the Gods. Someone I recently gave a job to. Someone I'm not overly proud of avoiding most of the time. I'm just going to have to find her...when the sun comes back up.

CHAPTER 3

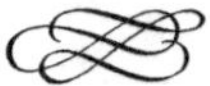

I think you know someone who can lead you straight to
them.

$\mathcal{I}$ knew exactly who he meant. There was only one
person I knew who was that devoted to her religion, even when it kept her from getting what she wanted
most. When we called for more people in the war, Jasper was
one of them. Jasper was Kit's best friend. I didn't know him
well, but I knew the people he mattered to the most. It was
when I looked at the list of people who perished, in order to
send condolences to their families that I found out. Beatrice
was in tears when I saw her. I, on the other hand, was
drowning in guilt. That's when I knew. 'He felt so bad after
those men came for his debts. He wanted to do something to
make me proud. But I was already proud of him. He's been
taking care of me since I was just a child. I was three years of
age and he looked out for me, fed me, protected me. How can

you not be proud of someone like that?' She cried and all I could do was apologize. She didn't blame me though. She didn't blame anyone. That's what her belief gave her. The ability to believe death was something natural.

There was still something I could do for her. The only thing I could do for her to try and make up for everything. I gave her a job. She was on her own now and she had to find a way to make money. The castle was too far for her to make the journey back home, but by finding her a job with the castle servants, they were able to provide her a place to sleep until she had enough money to rent a servant room in the castle, or a house of her own closer than the last.

But every Sunday, she made one journey without fail. She walked an hour to a farm that let her rent a horse, and from there, all the way towards her old temple for worship. I'd seen her make the travel in rain and storm, heat and cold. Whatever it took, she went.

She came back this Sunday early in the afternoon. Her long, black hair was tightly braided back, her light-brown skin—a shade darker from the walks in the sun—were in perfect contrast to the soft, light-colored dresses she liked to wear. Her eyes—they were dark before, but now they were almost black from her grief. She told me once that every loss in her life made her eyes a shade darker. I understood.

Beatrice smiled when she saw me standing near the side entrance of the castle. It was the closest one to the servants' section, and therefore less busy than the one more direct. "What do I owe the pleasure of having the Princess waiting for me?" Beatrice asked, slightly bowing her head. She always bowed her head, no matter how many times I asked her not to.

"I was hoping you would join me for an afternoon snack. I know you tend to skip lunch."

"I would rather enjoy that."

I nodded, walking inside with her. We walked into my personal living room right next to my bedroom, where I was able to spend time either by myself or with someone I needed to get information from. I had asked Abbey to send sandwiches and the tea I like, so it was waiting for us when we got there. It was always more food than any one person could need, but with the coronation coming, Grace wanted to know every party food I liked and didn't. This was probably the only part of this whole situation I didn't complain about.

My living room was made of mainly whites and a couple hints of red. It was more basic than I would have picked, but I did find a sense of calm in the colors. We walked over to the table where there were plate towers—one held four layers of different fingers sandwiches, another, four different fruits, a plate of three types of cheeses, and our tea waiting for us. "Eat as much as you like. I have to keep a list of foods I like, and they always send way too much," I explained, taking my seat before Beatrice would take hers.

"Is this for the coronation?" Beatrice asked, picking up a slice of cheese.

I picked up two tea glasses, filling them with tea. "Yes, with all the classes I am taking, sitting for a food testing would take too much time." I slightly shrugged. "Plus, I really didn't want to do that. I don't want to have a party at all."

"A coronation isn't a party," Beatrice spoke with a mouth full of a cheddar-pickle sandwich.

"I've been told. How do you like your tea?"

"Two sugars please."

I finished up her tea as instructed before setting it by her, making mine as I liked. I picked up a salmon-cucumber, examining the little triangle. "I've had a lot of time to think since the war," I said, taking a soft bite of the sandwich.

"Thinking of ways for me to fix some things. Right some wrongs."

"What do you mean?"

"With all the magic in the world, don't you think there should be a way to…keep people from dying like that? Keep people from dying when they shouldn't."

Beatrice paused for a moment, thinking as she chewed her food. "We aren't supposed to have the power to stop death," Beatrice slightly shrugged.

"Kit wasn't supposed to die." I felt myself snap, pressing my lips together.

Beatrice chuckled, "Kit more than anyone would hate the idea of being able to stop death. He was fine with the magic that made life a little safer, especially when the dark forest started spreading, but as far as stopping a natural part of life, he wouldn't even stop to think about it."

A sharp feeling moved through my chest as I suddenly became less hungry. What if he didn't understand why I did whatever I had to do to get him back? What if he didn't need to come back? What if there was something like peace and he had found it?

"I don't know if you know this, but Anna created the dark forest because she was weakening the veil."

Beatrice nodded, picking up some fruit, "I heard. The servants know a lot."

I nodded, taking a drink of my tea, "Had me thinking a lot about how it was made it the first place."

Beatrice slightly nodded, visibly swallowing hard. I took notice of the way her eyes glanced around the marble table, her leg quickly dancing under the table, and the slow motion of her jaw after she quickly shoved a sandwich in her mouth. Beatrice looked up to see me carefully staring at her, and she swallowed the food in her mouth. "You live with the biggest library in Neville. I'm sure you can find a book on the subject."

"I know, but the book I want isn't there."

"There are many books in the library," she answered quickly as she drank her tea.

"Do you know what book I may be looking for?"

Beatrice quickly shook her head, but she didn't look at me and the way she itched her brow told me that she was lying. About what, was the question.

I couldn't push too hard. If I pushed too hard, she could ask questions I couldn't answer. I push too hard, and she could catch on to what I wished to do. She would tell someone and then what would I do? How would I stop her? I could put her in with Anna, but then what would Anna do to her? There's only one thing I could possibly do.

I kept my mouth shut, picking up another sandwich, letting the conversation move onto something lighter.

I SWUNG OPEN the magic door as I stormed into the room where Anna was reading a book from the small bookshelf hanging on the wall. "I have a problem," I admitted, shutting the door behind me and sliding down to the floor. I left my legs stretched out in front of me. I didn't even realize how tired I really was until my head rested back against the door.

"You haven't found the book?" Anna asked, shutting the book in her lap.

I sighed, "I think Beatrice knows where it is, but I can't ask her. I can't ask anyone. I can't talk to anyone but you. I don't want to talk to you. I don't even like you."

Anna paused for a moment, letting out a deep breath, "Are you done whining?"

I groaned, using my hands to rub my tired eyes, "I don't even know why I came here!"

"Because you have no one else. What does it say about someone who was alone most of her life and would then choose to isolate herself from everyone around her? Even when it means having to talk to the person you don't even like?"

"You talk too much."

Anna rolled her eyes, "Just give her a truth tea. It's not hard. She won't be able to lie for 24 hours, it will make her very suggestible, and she won't remember anything tomorrow if you slip in a nightcrawler leaf. Only one unless you want her sleeping for weeks on end."

"I'm not going to drug my friend."

"If she was a friend, you would be willing to tell her the truth and you wouldn't be here."

How could I argue with that? I couldn't. She wasn't my friend. She was the sister to the best friend of the man I lost. I was helping her because her brother died. I could say that it was because of me. I could say it was because Anna went crazy. I could tell myself that all of this could have been avoided, but I didn't know that. The only thing that I did know was how much I needed that book.

It's wrong.

I could probably break her without any drugs.

I can't trust what Anna says.

I don't know the consequences this tea will have.

I could come up with a list of reasons why this whole thing was a bad idea, but somehow none of that seemed good enough. None of them stopped me from going down to the kitchen.

I told them I wished to be alone, and that's exactly what

they gave me… one perk I rather enjoyed. I set the water to heat while I crushed together a single nightcrawler leaf and the rest of the herbs in the small, dark mortar.

Once the herbs had enough time to soak into the water, I brought the tea to my bedroom and into my closet. I didn't normally drink tea in my closet, but I would when I needed someone to come up and tailor the dress I ripped.

I set the tray down, hearing a knock on my bedroom door. I let Beatrice into my room and into my closet to show her the dress. All she saw was the tear at the bottom of the skirt. She moved a small stool next to the stand holding the dress, setting her needles and thread next to her. "Would you like some tea?" I asked after a while as she examined the tear in the dress.

"I shouldn't while I'm handing a needle," Beatrice smirked.

So, I waited until she was almost done with the dress before walking over to pour her a cup of the special tea, holding my breath as I handed it over.

"Thank you."

I turned away like I was going to be pouring myself a glass too, but instead I was giving her time to drink hers. It was supposed to work immediately. I could feel my heart racing. This had to be one of the worst things I had ever done, but she wouldn't remember it. "How are you feeling?" I asked, trying to keep my hands from shaking.

Beatrice sighed, "Honestly, I'm exhausted. I try to do everything right, but I feel like I'm running in circles."

I turned around to look at her and she seemed completely unaware of her honesty. I had to start light. "What happened to your parents?" I said 'light' Maisey!

Beatrice shrugged, "Daddy died just after I was born. He worked in construction and there was an accident. Don't know much about it. Just what Jasper was willing to tell me.

Mama couldn't leave her bed after that. All she did was cry. Eventually, her heart just gave up." She was so casual when she spoke— there was no way the tea wasn't working. I would be worried if it wasn't.

"I need to know where the book is," I said, clasping my hands in front of me—the way Grace did when she was being forceful yet trying to pretend it was a gentle suggestion.

Beatrice looked at me, unfazed by my questioning, "What book?"

"The journal of Lady Ophelia."

She nodded, "Father Gregory asked for it. Said he had some answers that he needed to find."

"About what?"

Beatrice let out a large yawn, rolling her head around her shoulders, "You don't ask. You have faith." Her eyes softly shut like she was about to take a nap on the floor.

"Come with me," I stepped closer, picking up her arm, and brought her into my bedroom. "I want you to get some sleep. We spent so much time together, and I just let you stay for the night."

She got into my bed without question or hesitation, "That's so nice of you."

I let out a deep breath, pulling the blanket over her. Her breathing was calm as she fell into a deep sleep. "Yeah, so nice of me," I whispered, trying my best to ignore the guilt rising inside of me.

I'll make sure she's okay.

I got my answer.

I'm one step closer to getting what I need.

I'm one step closer to Kit. That is what matters.

. . .

THERE WERE TOO many pros to go back now. I would get the book, and then I would make this up to her as well. I would do whatever I had to do to get Kit back. When that was all over, I would fix everything that I broke! I could do both. I would do both. I had to do both.

CHAPTER 4

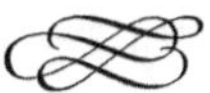

Morning came and I was standing by the balcony, my red robe tied tightly around my body as I heard Beatrice starting to stir in my bed. "My head," she groaned, pushing herself up. "What happened?" Beatrice turned around to look at me. Her eyes got wide as she quickly jumped out of my bed. "I am so sorry, Princess!" She moved to make my bed and I quickly shook my head.

"Please stop," I practically begged, and she froze, looking back at me. "And what did we say about the princess nonsense."

Beatrice sighed as she softly nodded, "I knew you before you were a princess, so the rules don't apply."

I nodded.

Beatrice paused, tightly pressing her lips together. "I still don't understand what happened."

Come on, Maisey! You practiced this! "Well, I ripped my dress, and you came up to fix it. You weren't feeling well. I called to get you some medicine. The fever got you a little loopy and eventually I just put you in my bed before you passed out in the hallway."

Beatrice looked away, trying to search her own memories. "I don't remember feeling sick."

"I'm not surprised. A twenty-four-hour sickness can just wipe a person out."

Beatrice slightly nodded. Whether she believed it or not, she was going to make herself believe it. She looked back at me with a soft smile, "Thank you for taking such good care of me."

"What are friends for?" They aren't for drugging you, manipulating you, and then lying to you.

Beatrice walked out of my bedroom, leaving me to kick myself and my own reckless thoughts. I would have plenty of time to feel guilty, but not today. Today I had things to handle. Today I was going to get the journal of Lady Ophelia.

I HEARD some things about Father Gregory, but not much. There wasn't too much to say. He was one of the youngest leaders to gain their own parish so quickly—only twenty-eight, his predecessor having died two years ago. Some people rather enjoyed the change that came with following a young leader, but others preferred the slower pace of an older priest. I tried to ask around about him, but all I really got was how great it was I was diving into religion. Once I got tired of hearing that, I decided to stop asking. Whatever I was going to be meeting was just going to have to be a surprise.

Unlike Beatrice, I had a horse and learning to ride her was one of the first things I did after the war. Grace thought it would make me feel better. I only did it because they didn't have cars in Neville, and I wasn't going to ride with someone else. They didn't even have roads in some parts of the kingdom. Someone just decided to walk in a direction and others followed and they called that a road. I couldn't even imagine the struggles when it rained. Leaving the castle grounds wasn't something Grace was fond of me doing.

I put on riding pants and had my hair braided over my shoulder for the journey, making it easier for such a taxing ride. I made it to the small, dark stone chapel decorated with stained-glass windows. I got down off the horse, taking the rope to tie her up to a post. The chapel was empty from the looks of it, which worked in my favor as I entered the room. Father Gregory stood in front of the altar of candles, dressed in a long black robe with a white collar. His hair was dark brown, and his skin was tanned from a lot of time in the sun. "You've traveled very far," Father Gregory spoke with a thick accent, one unlike any other I had noticed.

"Where are you from? I haven't been able to learn how to recognize accents yet."

He chuckled, turning around to face me with a small, less than welcoming, smile on his face, "I am from across the ocean. A beautiful island blessed by the Gods."

"If it's blessed, why did you leave?"

"I wanted to spread the Gods' love."

"Does that including having Beatrice steal the journal of Lady Ophelia?"

He chuckled again, holding his hands behind his back as he stepped closer to me by a few steps. "I did not know she stole it. I simply wished to keep something so strong protected, and she brought it to me of her own free will."

I scoffed, "So, your power, seeing how you are the leader of her faith, had no influence on her doing something so out of character?"

"Princess, I don't like what you are implying."

"I don't like a man using his power to manipulate people that trust him."

"The journal of Lady Ophelia is a very powerful piece of our past and it can't be trusted with just anyone."

"And it should be trusted to you?"

"I work for the Gods. Everything I do is for them. I don't have ulterior motives." Suggestion was all over his tone, and I felt my entire body tense.

"I am the Princess of Neville and the journal is our property. I want it back. Now."

I could tell he was getting antsy, moving his head. I noticed the slight glance towards the door in the back. He tried to cover it up as if he was just debating how to answer me, but I'd had to rely on my ability to read people for most of my life. Father Gregory looked over at me, clearing his throat, "I can't give it to you."

It had been a long time since someone told me no here, but this wasn't a situation where I could take no for an answer. I lifted my chin slightly, dismissing his statement as I looked in his eyes, "I wasn't asking." I moved past him, my shoulder nudging his.

"Princess, you must stop. This is sacred ground, ruled by the Gods not by you." He followed me as I barged through the door into a separate room. It was clearly an office, judging by the desk with shelves behind it piled with papers and books. A painting of an older man, probably the last priest, hung on the wall.

It has to be in here somewhere.

"You must leave at once!" The priest shouted at me, and my eyes heated up in a rage-filled fire.

I didn't know what I was expecting to do with him. I whipped around, thrusting my hand towards him, and a ball of power generating from my hand into him. He ran across the room and slammed against the wall before falling to the ground. I closed my hand, the color quickly leaving my face. "I didn't...I didn't mean to." I rushed towards him, but he didn't stir. I moved down, pressing my fingers against his neck to feel a fast pulse. I let out a deep breath. At least he was alive. I wouldn't have to add the murder of a priest to the things I'd done.

I stood back up, looking around the room. There had to be a safe somewhere in this room. He was hiding the book. He didn't want me to have it. I let out a deep breath, trying to think of where I would hide it. He wouldn't want anyone to find it, but he would want it close.

Maisey. Maisey. A tingle went down my spine and my heart started to race. Maisey. Maisey. My eyes heated up again like they were reaching out for something. I felt my feet start to move on their own towards the painting on the wall. I took down the painting, having to brace myself at the heavy weight of it. The gold frame must be actual gold because this is the heaviest fu— I stumbled slightly, dropping the painting a few inches to the ground before leaning it against the wall. I sighed, looking back at the wall to see a gap. I crammed my finger in the hole, wiggling the brick until it stuck out far enough for me to grab it. I pulled out the brick, setting it on the desk. I could see the journal lying in a rather large hole with brown bags and pieces of gold coins surrounding it. I carefully grabbed the journal when a groan came from behind me. I turned around to see Father Gregory slowly pushing himself up off the floor.

He stumbled, trying to catch his balance, "You have no idea the power in that journal."

"I know exactly the power that is in that journal."

"Lady Ophelia did more than create the veil between our world and the next. She used power so dark that it corrupts everyone that it touches. She was able to save her soul before she did anything too drastic, but you are not as pure-souled as her. You will damn Neville and everyone in it!"

I took a threatening step forward, "I am saving Neville! You wouldn't know what that is like, and I am warning you to stay out of my way."

"You do this, and you will be no greater than your devil of an aunt!"

All I saw was red. Nothing but red-hot rage. The only thing I could feel was my whole body shaking—it was a miracle my knees didn't give up right then. The fog slowly cleared enough for me to see Father Gregory up against the wall, his feet dangling off the ground and his hands at his throat trying to grab my mist of magic strangling the life out of him. His face turned red, and tears started rolling down his cheeks. "Watch what you say to me," I spoke through my teeth, watching him gasp for air. I lowered my hand, dropping him to the ground with a thud. He coughed and gasped, trying to get as much air back as he could. When he looked back up at me all I could see was the terror. As if he was looking at the eyes of a monster. And maybe he was. "You say a word and it will be the last thing you do."

He vigorously nodded and I held the journal close to my chest as I walked out of the chapel.

THE ENTIRE RIDE, I listened to the journal whispering my name. It made my magic stir like rapid waves in the ocean. Danger and chaos mixed together. I brought the horse back into the barn, keeping the journal hidden under my shirt as I walked up the stairs to my studio. Once inside, I shut the door quickly, setting the journal on the table and grabbing a chair for the door, as usual. The pages of the journal were thick and wrinkled with age but every page was solid. It was so well-preserved that you couldn't even rip the pages out of the binding of the journal. The words on the cover were only shadows of what they had been centuries ago. I turned to the first page, and on the slightly yellow-tinted pieces of paper were dark words. Not a single piece of the writing was missing. But something was wrong. I flipped page after page. I went through every single one finding the same problem on every single page. I couldn't read a single word of it! I slammed my fist against the table, fighting the urge to scream. I wasn't supposed to be stuck relying on Anna anymore, but someone had to read it.

When I looked up from the table, the door to Anna's room was wide open, giving me a full view of her. She walked over, standing in the doorway of the room. "Can't read it, can you?" Anna asked with a smirk on her face.

"You knew I wouldn't be able to read it," I snapped.

Anna slightly shrugged, "I had a feeling, but I don't know anything until I try it."

"How. Do. I. Read. It?"

"You're going to need to find someone who can realm travel and I don't know how to help you with that." I waved the door to slam it shut in her face. It took everything I had not to throw the book and her across the room.

CHAPTER 5

hy would I rely on Anna alone for information? I couldn't. She was a crazy person who liked to lie for fun. I would have to be a complete idiot to believe everything she told me. Clearly, I couldn't read the book, but she was not the only person in Neville that might be able to tell me what I was looking for. I took a piece of paper, copying a line from the journal. I didn't know what it said, or even if the line was complete. But I copied every mark of the line before picking up the journal and walking back over to the basket I had in the corner. It was filled with a nicely folded white blanket and books, so when I placed the journal there, it would be less likely to stand out. I walked out of my study, locking the door behind me, and made my way down the stairs of the tower.

It didn't take too long to make it to Tasar's office. I knocked on the door, waiting for him to open it. I knew he was in there by the noise.

Stumble, Curse, Crash — Stumble, Curse, Crash — Stumble, Curse, Crash!

Until the door finally swung open. Tasar looked like a

mess. His naturally tan skin was pale, his white hair spiked in all directions, and his brown eyes had sunken with exhaustion. "You look awful," I stated, barging in his office.

"So glad to see you," Tasar mumbled, shutting the door behind me, and I looked around his office. I was used to the cluttered mess when I came in here, but this was up ten notches. The books and papers seemed to have doubled to the point some were even on the floor, including a table from one of the many crashes.

"This place is a mess," I turned to look at him, seeing Tasar rubbing his eyes. "What is going on?"

"For me to become leading physician and lead medical adviser before the acting one steps down, I need to cram for the test." Tasar walked past me, picking up some books off the floor.

I crossed my arms. "I think you are more than qualified."

"Well, that means a lot, truly, but that doesn't change the fact most people don't like the idea of me becoming lead anything."

"Why not?"

"Pick your choice," Tasar scoffed. "I'm too young, I'm too arrogant, I'm too Elvin, I'm too ill-bred—" Tasar stopped, pressing his lips together as if he said more than he intended to. Instead, he just sighed, walking over to plop down in a chair. "What can I help you with?"

I let out a deep breath, handing the note over to him, "I need you to try and translate this."

Tasar took the letter, staring at it, his eyes narrowing the longer he looked at it. "What is this?" Tasar asked, not bothering to look at me.

"It's a piece of an old book I found in the library. I wanted to read it, but I can't make anything out."

Tasar looked up at me, confused, "What book?"

I slightly shrugged, "I couldn't read the name." Liar. Liar. Pants on fire.

Tasar looked at it one more time before sighing and giving it back to me, "Well, I can't read this."

I tried to hide my irritation, hopefully if he saw it, he linked it to disappointment.

"I don't think there are many people that can."

I looked back at him, "What do you mean?"

"From what I could tell, its multiple languages melded together in what is called realm language. The only people that can read it are those who can travel between worlds and are strong enough to pick up on languages. It's rare because it's so dangerous and a lot of work. Couldn't tell you where you could find one."

I sighed, racking my brain on who could possibly— Kit! I looked over at Tasar, who was staring at me with complete interest. "Thank you for your help," I said, walking out of the room and shutting the door behind me. Memories flooded back, and I tried to replay Kit's words.

"...Julianne...She knows everything from flowers to magic, not just in this world..."

Tears welled in my eyes. Not because I couldn't remember everything. I remembered enough. It was the fact the words appeared in my head as my own voice. I couldn't remember his anymore. He was fading away, and if I didn't hurry, he was going to be lost forever. Soon, would I forget everything? The feeling I got from him. The natural feeling of safety in a way I couldn't understand. In a way I never felt before. A feeling I would never have again.

My lip started to quiver as a tear slid down my cheek, and I quickly wiped it away. First it was the feeling of his touch. His hands were large and rough from all his work, but not in a way that was unpleasant. It was just the opposite. Every touch was soft and concerned. Every touch told me that he cared, even when I tried so hard to shut myself off from him.

The feeling of his lips against mine took longer to fade, but it too was a distant memory. I knew the feelings that it gave me, but I couldn't describe it. It was good, it was everything it was supposed to be, and so much more.

I choked on a sob trying to break the surface. I quickly put my hand over my mouth, rushing into a room before anyone could notice. I scanned the room to see it was empty. "Stop it. Stop it. Stop it." I whispered to myself, squeezing my eyes shut to stop the tears. I leaned against the door, using it to keep myself upright. My heartbreak came out in a devastated laugh. One memory and I was falling apart. "Idiot. Pathetic. Weak." I wiped my face with my shaking hands. I took a deep breath in and let it out. "Maisey Collins, princess or not, you have work to do! Pull yourself together! Your future happiness depends on it!" I quickly shook my head, focusing on one thing and one thing only.

Finding Julianne.

Now, I didn't have days to get all the way back to the Inn. Not only was I completely sure there was no way I could leave for days without it being noticed, but I didn't even know where it was located. I did know what the room looked like, and I knew something that would get me there in the blink of an eye.

I was able to swipe two little orange balls from the weapons room, and I would be there and back before anyone noticed I was gone. I thought about the room I was in before. The bench with a black sheet over the window, the wood floors with a multi-colored rug on the floor, and dresses, shoes, and mirrors for the women to use. I tossed one of the balls onto the ground of my bedroom, opening a portal to the room. I stepped inside, letting it close behind me. The room was exactly how I remembered it, and it was also empty. Well, it was until the door opened and a young woman with curly red hair, marks on her neck, and her dress halfway off walked into the room. "Who are you?" the young lady asked, trying to decide if I was one of her or not, "You c-can't be in here."

"Bring me Alice," I demanded, and she stared at me stunned. "Now!" Her eyes got wide before she scurried down the hall.

I walked over, sitting down on the bench. It only took five minutes to see Alice running up the stairs with the worried girl behind her. She stopped in the hall when she saw me. She looked the same, but different. Her once long, dark-brown hair was now cut to her shoulders. Her blue eyes were slightly darker in a way I hadn't noticed before. Now that I thought about it, I realized I hadn't really looked at her eyes before. Her dress was way more revealing than before, so much so that it was hard to notice anything else. Alice slightly smiled, said something to the girl that got her to go into another room, and joined me in the dressing room. She shut the door before crossing her arms, "They told me someone appeared with demands. I didn't expect it to be royalty."

I slightly smiled, standing up from the bench, "I need your help."

Alice looked at me sternly, "Last time you were here you smacked one of the men with a bottle. Hasn't been back here since." She paused for a moment before cracking a smile and laughing, "I'll do anything for you. Guy was a pig. Plus, I heard about Kit. Tobyn was in here sobbing. I'm sorry."

I swallowed hard, "Last time I was here, Kit talked to a woman named Julianne. Said she knew things about different worlds. I need to see her."

Alice nodded, "Follow me." Alice led me out of the bedroom to the first door on the right, "But I will warn you, I don't think you are going to find what you are looking for." She opened the door, letting me inside.

I walked into the room, there was only one candle by the bed. I walked over to see a woman with dark skin, her hair wrapped up in a red silk flowered wrap with a couple of black curls out around her face. She was so peaceful, but chaotic at the same time. Like a wave of energy was coming off her. I reached over, lightly touching her arm. I instantly made note of how cold she was. Touching her was like holding ice in my hands. I looked over, "How long has she been like this?" I asked and Alice sighed.

"Since the war," Alice walked over to the other side of the bed, taking Julianne's hand and brushing her cheek with the back of her finger. "People told her not to cross while the magic here was so unstable. Then...that gust of magic radiated through the kingdom. She screamed, spoke a language I didn't understand, and she's been like this ever since."

"You really cared about her."

Alice nodded, "I care for all the girls. They deserve to be loved even if the rest of the world doesn't see that. If she wakes up, I want her to know she was cared for." Alice let out a deep breath before motioning her head towards the two piles of books sitting on the floor across the room, "We still have her books. I'm assuming that's why you needed her."

I nodded, "Get them and let's go."

Alice looked up at me with wide eyes, "Go?"

"You know her well enough to get me everything I need, and I can't possibly carry those books by myself."

Alice chuckled, slightly shaking her head, "They don't let women like me in the castle."

"They will if I tell them to."

Alice didn't really look that convinced, but she didn't argue with me. I didn't know if Alice believed me, if she just knew I wasn't going to let it go, if she wanted to see if I was right, or if she just wanted to come, but either way she agreed to go. She told one of the girls they were in charge until she came back, gave her a list of responsibilities, and grabbed her half of the books. I used the beads to transport us back into my bedroom.

Alice looked around the room with wide eyes and jaw to the floor, "I knew the rooms in the castle would be beautiful." I walked over to the table, setting the books down with a loud thud. One of these books had to help me, and I would be reading them all if I had to.

I spent two days reading the books while Alice had fun, dressing in my clothes, sleeping in my bed, eating my food, and roaming the halls. I didn't know what she did when she left my room, but she always came back with a smile. I rather enjoyed when she left, only because I could feel her staring at me when she was here. She didn't ask any questions, but I could feel them burning into me. Yet, I also didn't want her to leave. I wasn't entirely sure why, but it was just another thing on my list of things to avoid talking about.

It was halfway through the third day that Grace decided to pay me a visit. She walked into the room without knocking, clearly unhappy about something. "You've been reading," she said, clasping her hands in front of her. "For three days?"

I sighed, "I know I missed some classes—"

"And meetings and coronation planning. You can't avoid your responsibilities."

"I'm not."

"And don't think I don't know who has been roaming our halls during the day. You have a harlot in my castle!"

I held my breath and all the comments floating to the surface, "Her name is Alice and she's a friend. Listen, I am sorry that I missed my appointments, and I will try to remember that, but Alice stays."

"Why do you care?"

It was a fair question, but the answer didn't come out as easily as it probably should have. "I don't know," I admitted. "She helped me when I first got here. She was friends with Kit," I looked up at Grace, noticing the way she arched her brows at me. "Not like that, but..." I tried to put a finger on what I was feeling, but I didn't have one clue. Maybe I was trying to hold onto things that linked me to a time before I knew this kind of loss. "I don't know."

Grace stared at me for a moment, her eyes scanning my face before hers softened, "Alright then. She can stay, but you are responsible for her. You need to have someone make a room for her until we find a place for her, preferably a job, and certainly some clothing. She's not the same size as you and with breasts that large it's hard to go unnoticed when the dress doesn't fit right."

I nodded slightly, "Thank you."

The door swung open as Alice walked back into the room, freezing when she saw Grace. I swear the color left her face before she bowed. "I'm so sorry to interrupt, my Queen."

Grace smiled at Alice with the smile she gave everyone in the castle, "It's no trouble. Welcome to the castle, Alice." I swear I saw her cringe slightly, but she played it off well enough before walking out of the room.

Alice waited for the door to shut before looking back at me with arched brows, "Welcome?"

I shrugged, looking down at my book. What are you even doing? I didn't know. At this point I think it would have taken ten experts to understand what was going on in my head.

. . .

ALICE HAD a habit of spending her days roaming the castle halls, and no matter how hard I tried, the only thing these books did was replay every bad thing I'd done to get what I needed. It could have been the fact my eyes were burning, or my head was pounding, or my body screaming for some sense of relief. I just needed a break. A break and some tea.

I sat on the couch of my bedroom as Beatrice brought in the tea I asked for. She was dressed in a beautiful blue dress with butterflies moving up her skirt. She looked nicer than any other servant in the castle, but bringing tea wasn't part of her job anymore. Beatrice set my tray down on the table, filling my cup, including milk and sugar. She handed me the cup and I motioned towards one of the chairs. "Sit."

Beatrice didn't hesitate to sit in the chair with a smile. "I tried to thank you sooner." Beatrice pointed out. "I know you had me transferred to the position of castle seamstress."

"Well, I knew how much you liked dresses, and I thought it could be a good change." Was that true? Yes, but it was also filled with guilt.

"You know, most people would have sent me on my way, and I would be either living under the church or working in the Inn. Neither are what I wanted, and I can see why Kit cared about you so much."

I felt my brows furrow as I looked at her. "Did he say something to you?"

Beatrice chuckled. "Kit never said much of anything. The only way to read him, just like my brother, was in his eyes. They seemed to shine brighter when he looked at you." Beatrice paused for a moment, the tension going thick in the room as I thought about him. As I tried to picture his face. As I tried to see if I ever noticed what she saw. "How is your new friend?"

I looked up at her, trying to remember whether I ever

introduced them or not. "She is enjoying herself. Have you two met?"

I noticed the way her body tensed as she gripped her hands together in her lap. "No. I wouldn't know someone like that." Beatrice took a deep breath in, pushing herself up from her chair and brushed her, obviously clean, skirt. "I just remembered some work I must complete. May I be excused?"

"Don't let me stand in your way." I said, and she bowed slightly before walking out of the room. I understood wanting to keep a part of your past secret. I had a fair share of things that I wouldn't tell anyone else. But that didn't stop a little nagging voice in the back of my head that wanted to know more. I could imagine. Hell, I probably already knew.

CHAPTER 6

My eyes were burning, my eyelids were heavy, my body was screaming from being in the same position for hours. I wanted to say that looking at these books was finally giving me answers, but they weren't even words anymore. They were lines and shapes molding together, falling apart, and coming off the page. They were trying to attack me, circling me like a shark circles its dinner. I put my hands on my head to keep it from exploding when the book slammed shut in front of me. I jumped, looking up to see Alice looking down at me with a plate in her hand. "I flirted with the cook to get us this," Alice moved the plate closer to me and I was hit with the warm smell of peanut butter cookies. "A little birdie told me they were your favorites."

I sighed, "One can't hurt." I reached over to grab a cookie when Alice swiped the plate away from me.

"You can have one out on the balcony. You stare any longer at those books, your eyes are going to cross. I saw a man that had crossed eyes once; he ran into everything. I don't even know how he made it into the Inn," Alice shook her head, picking up one of the cookies as she stepped out onto the balcony.

I opened the book, looking at the words—no, symbols! This wasn't working! I cursed, slamming the book shut before standing up from the table. I walked out to the balcony to find Alice sitting in one of the chairs. She just stared out into the distance as I walked over to sit in the chair next to hers. The second my butt hit the chair the plate was in front of me. I smiled, picking up the warm cookie and holding it in my hand. I broke pieces off, placing the taste of it on my tongue.

"I saw Beatrice in the castle," Alice said, breaking the silence between us.

I nodded slightly, looking over at her. "When I talked to her, it seemed like you two knew each other."

Alice nodded, looking out at the distance in front of us. "You should go to her for this story."

"Maybe but I'm asking you, and you're the one who brought it up."

"Beatrice didn't run to God because of who she loved. She did it because she got her heart broken."

There was only one way they were going to run into each other. I remembered going to Beatrice's house. It was basically isolated with only woods surrounding it. "By a girl who worked with you."

"Yes. The Inn was the only place she could actually find Jasper because the game doesn't allow women to step inside. Maxie protected her. Kept her company. She fell in love with Maxie, and Maxie loved her."

"What happened?"

"Beatrice wanted a future, but Maxie was never going to stop working. Then Maxie got sick and died before Beatrice could say goodbye. Beatrice was broken-hearted, never wanting to love again to the point it changed who she was. Ran all the way to that priest of hers. If it was up to him, I would be burned at the stake, only men would sit at the throne, the church would have the ultimate power over the kingdom, and we would be sacrificing our first-born daughters." Alice let out a bitter laugh. "Can you imagine? We are good enough for the Gods, but not good enough to lead. Anyway, Beatrice started to believe it was her love that killed Maxie. You couldn't convince her otherwise. Jasper tried, but after she had run away because of it he vowed never to bring up again. She found her peace in his hate. Punished herself for something that wasn't her fault."

"And seeing you reminds her of Maxie." I spoke quietly, looking down at the cookie in my hands.

Alice broke the short silence between us as I ate my cookie. "Sadly, we can't control how people see us. As you know, I've met a lot of people, but none of them have changed as much as you have. Gods know, I wouldn't have seen that coming."

"What do you mean?" I asked, turning to look at her as she stared at the view.

Alice's face was serious, a slight clench in her jaw as she was thinking so hard, "You're changing people. We all know who we are supposed to be. The roles we are meant to fill. Yet, here we are, a princess sitting next to a person like me, dressed as a lady, inside the castle walls."

"Well, rules are meant to be broken."

Alice smiled, chuckling slightly before looking over at me, "You want to tell me why you've been staring at the books so long?"

I sighed, putting the last of the cookie in my mouth and looking back at the beautiful night sky. A part of me wanted to tell her everything. I wanted to tell someone, so I could talk to someone—anyone other than Anna. But even though I didn't think Alice would judge me, I couldn't risk what I would have to do if she didn't take what I had to say well. Father Gregory tried to get hostile against me, and I almost killed him. What if I couldn't stop myself this time? What if I took it too far and I couldn't take it back? I held my breath, turning to look at her, "A princess is supposed to learn as much as she can."

"Yes, but realm traveling isn't normal practice."

"And you would know that?"

"Men like to talk when they are satisfied."

I chuckled, shaking my head, "My powers have been unstable since I stepped foot in Neville. The better I understand why it has the strength it does, the better chance of protecting people from it."

"Well, you are doing something right because you look much better than before."

I slightly nodded, remembering back.

…my red hair was turning white, why my skin was getting paler, why even my green eyes were losing color.

I knew that it wasn't all in my head. I knew it was something bigger, even when the doctors couldn't find it. I was in a world where, not only did I not believe in it, magic simply did not exist and science couldn't give me an answer. I was just left floating in the void of confusion, as if I was paying the price for a crime I committed in a past life. In reality, the only crime I was paying for was the fact I was born. Another thing I had no power over. Something completely out of my control. I spent the first half of my life struggling through things that were out of my control.

Growing up, I knew a few things from the file I read on my case worker's desk. I was waiting for her to find me a new foster family, and I was snooping. I was ten. She should have seen it coming. My entire ten years were filled with people telling me I was cursed, evil, bad luck, and, worst of all, I believed them. It was hard not to. I wasn't not entirely convinced I'm not still.

We can't control how people see us.

The file said I was left all alone when I was a few months old in an alley between a gym and a coffee shop, and only three buildings down from a hospital in Chicago. All I knew was that my parents clearly ignored their options and chose to throw me away. I tried to live with that. I tried to accept it, move on, and make them sorry for throwing me away. That was easier said than done.

Then I made the mistake of pushing even further for a project in school where we had to talk about our past. I knew I could talk to my teacher and find some way out of it. I was in my tenth foster home, and I wasn't looking to explain why I was moving around so much. So, I talked to my caseworker —no, I begged my caseworker, "There has to be more! I know that can't be it! My parents abandoned me! That is a crime! I need to know more!" My begging worked with the only person that even seemed to like me.

She did warn me. She told me that just because you feel the need to know more, doesn't always mean you should. I knew she had to be right, but I was fifteen and I wasn't going to listen to her. Then I was left with a story that broke me all the way down to my soul. All because some nurse tried to take me home…

Leaving work late one night, a young nurse from the hospital was on her way to the bus stop, just like every night. It was the only way she had to get home. This time she heard a sound that would not only get her attention, but her mind. She heard a baby crying—screaming—for someone…anyone to hold them, feed them, take them out of the cold. Instead of taking the baby to the hospital, she wanted to take the baby home. She didn't think about it.

She said she looked at the baby and knew what she had to do. Like a voice whispered at her. She called for a taxi, using the last of her money, to avoid anyone she might have known.

While they were inside the taxi, not even a block away from where the baby was taken, a drunk driver got behind the wheel because he wanted something to eat. He thought he gave the bartender, his long-term friend, his keys when he knew he had too much to drink. When he stepped outside to think of where he could walk for food, he found his keys hiding in his jacket pocket. In the crash, the drunk driver went through the windshield and died before help even arrived. The taxi driver took most of the damage and because the driver was going so fast, he died on his way to surgery from internal damage. The nurse was left with a broken arm, some broken ribs, bruises, and scratches from using her body to shield the baby, who didn't have one scratch.

When the police showed up to talk to the nurse, she had no idea what came over her. She said this red light hit her, and she couldn't stop herself. "It was the baby's fault! It's the devil! THAT BABY IS EVIL!" Someone wrote that nonsense down!

Now, I was different. The same, but different. My hair was a medium red, it used to be darker, but the white wasn't going away without a fight. My hair got a little bit of its curl back, turning it into more of a wave. My eyes were greener too, Florence said that it matched the color of a fern. Not sure if I liked that, but there was nothing I could do either. My skin had a little bit of life to it, but, like everything else, would never be like it was before. My spells were better. I couldn't remember the last time I fainted. I wasn't stuck in bed shaking anymore.

I may have looked better, but I was plagued with a new nightmare.

Once Alice had gone to bed in the room right next to mine, I took the books up to my studio. It took me multiple trips, but I had no other plans and nights were ridiculously long. I opened the door, dropping the books on the floor near Anna's feet. "You are going to find a way for me to read that journal," I demanded.

Anna looked down at the books before flicking her gaze up at me, "These can't help you."

"I'm not playing this game again. You said I need someone who knows realm language. The person I had is in a coma, so tell me what to do or I swear—"

"Don't be so dramatic," Anna said, rolling her eyes. "You and I both know you aren't going to kill me until you at least get what you want." She arched her brows at me as if she was daring me to argue with her. Instead of giving in, I crossed my arms. "Wow, you really don't know how to have initiative, do you? You are going to have to become a realm traveler."

I stared at her for a moment to be sure she was serious, "I can't do that!"

"Your magic is unstable and only unstable people do realm traveling."

"What do I do?" I asked, ignoring the insult.

Anna pushed herself forward on the chair, flipping through the books until she found the book she was looking for. She flipped through a few pages before showing it to me. It was written in the Nevillian ancient language. Luckily, that was one language I knew enough of. I ran my fingers over the title of the page reading: 'A Traveler's Guide'. It was a spell. It was everything that I needed. I turned around to walk out the door when Anna's voice stopped me. "Proceed with caution."

I stopped, turning on my heels to look at her.

"Do you know what kills more than war?"

I scoffed. I'd heard that one before. "Love."

Anna slightly shrugged, "Good answer. In some arguments you may be right, but I was going for arrogance. And you, my dear, have plenty to go around. You are willing to risk the entire world around us just because you got your heart broken."

Guilt ran through me like a wave in the ocean, trying to push me down. Instead of letting it, I pressed my lips together, glaring at her. "Careful, Anna. Someone might mistake you for caring."

"Don't. Do you not recall what you said after I was put in here?" I simply rolled my eyes. "No one knows I'm here. I can kick, scream, but if something happens to you, I die in here. I believe your exact words were, 'That would be a shitty way to go.'"

I slightly shrugged, "Sounds like me." Knowing good and well those were my exact words. Then I walked out of the room. I was done with the entire conversation, and, because I had all the say, so was she.

I brought the book to the table to get a better look at the paper. 'Crossing between realms is a talent. One that if done incorrectly can leave the host stuck in the void between one realm and another. Their body becoming a prison to their traveling mind. A fate worse than death. I give you two pieces of advice: <u>never</u> do it alone and <u>only</u> if you must.' Flashes of Julianne pushed forward. Stuck in her bed, trapped. I'd been stuck in my bed before, and I didn't plan on doing that again. I was going to need help. Help from someone I could keep from stopping me. Someone that could understand why I was doing this the most.

Once the sun started to rise and the castle started to come alive, I walked down the hall looking for Beatrice. She lost her friend. She lost her brother. She lost her home. She lost her way of life. She had to understand where I was coming from. How could she not? I found her carrying a basket down the hall. She smiled at me, slightly bowing her head. "I need to ask you something," I blurted out, ignoring normal greetings.

Beatrice nodded, "Anything."

I looked around at the people passing us and motioned her over towards the windows. I opened my mouth to do my best to explain my situation, when no words came out. I pressed my lips back together, trying something different, "I read this story about the ability to break down the veil created for our world, and it had me wondering—"

"That is not something we need to wonder about," Beatrice cut me off, quickly shaking her head.

"But if someone did—"

Beatrice shook her head again, pressing her lips together as if she could burst into tears, "It would be horrible. I can't even think of something like that happening."

I held my breath softly nodding. I can't tell her. Telling her would have been my biggest mistake since I let Kit stay with me at the castle. "You're right," I said. "It's a beautiful day. I shouldn't be trying to ruin it."

I turned, about to walk away when she stopped me, "Didn't you want to ask me something?"

I shook my head as if I didn't stop her, "Nope." I walked down the hall, cursing myself for being so stupid. She believed they were in a better place. She was under the thumb of a man who hated me. She wouldn't be willing to sell her soul. She'll never understand.

If I couldn't get someone to understand on an emotional

level, maybe there was another way. Maybe I could get someone to understand me intellectually. That was the best option. I had the power to do that safely. No one would have to get hurt.

I knocked on the door to Tasar's office, waiting for him to open it. He looked better than the last time I saw him. Like he got a good night's sleep. I couldn't even remember what that was like. "I need your help," I blurted out before he could say a word.

He looked at me, confused, "How can I help?"

"I can't tell you here. I need you to come with me," I walked away knowing he would follow behind me. I led him up the back stairs, up the tower, stopping once we stood in front of my studio door. This was a lot to ask him. I knew that. I sighed, turning to look back at him, "What I am about to ask you…you don't have to agree. I am just trying to do this as safely as possible, and you are the smartest person I know. This is not a demand. I am not your princess asking. I am a friend."

Tasar looked like he couldn't decide between being scared or just plain confused. "What's behind this door?"

I held my breath, opening the door. My feet froze in place seeing a figure standing near the table with the book in her hands—Ophelia's journal, I had hidden—in her hands. Every thought I had vanished. I couldn't think. This wasn't supposed to happen.

Alice looked up at me, dropping the heavy book on the table, "You have some serious explaining to do."

CHAPTER 7

"You have some serious explaining to do."

"How did you even get in here?" I asked, stepping towards her with my hands turning into fists.

"I started thinking about why you would want these books and Julianne's help. Then I remembered Kit asking for her. He was trying to help you get home, and who better to get answers from than someone who realm travels. Then I realized…the look in your eyes, I've seen it—I've had it," Alice stepped closer to me and I saw the look in her eyes. She knows. If she didn't know, she had a pretty good idea.

"I am just doing what I have to do."

"No, you are doing something you can't come back from!"

"What the hell is going on?!" Tasar shouted, getting us both to look at him, still standing in the doorway.

"Tell him," Alice demanded. "If you are doing the right thing, you shouldn't have a problem telling him."

I held my breath. Telling him was the only choice I had, so that was what I was going to do. I walked over to Tasar, pulling him into the room and shutting the door behind him. Once the door was shut, I could finally hear how fast my heart was racing. My hands were shaking against the door. Every way this could go wrong played through my head like Christmas songs during the Holidays. "I-It was my fault." My voice cracked as tears welled in my eyes. I closed them, leaning my head against the solid door as hot tears fell from my eyes onto the floor. "I should have told him to leave when I had the chance. His brother left, and I should have forced him too, but I didn't. I didn't want to have to go through it all alone, and…he was all I had."

"Maisey, what are you planning?" Tasar said quietly, and I didn't hear any confusion, only worry. He was right to be worried.

I let out a deep breath, turning to lean my back against the wall, "I'm going to lower the veil long enough to get Kit back. He was killed by Anna's magic— magic that didn't belong to her. It trapped his soul. If I do this, I could get him back."

"You could also release every single bad thing trapped on the other side," Tasar stated. "You could destroy Neville and every other kingdom in the world!"

"You think I haven't thought of that!" I shouted. "I know what I am risking, and I wouldn't do it if I didn't have people that knew what they were doing."

"Who?"

"His name is Odes. He runs the veil on the other side. He's been helping me get Kit back, and he brought me—" I sighed, stopping myself. There was no easy way to say it. So, I lifted my hand, waving open the door. Tasar and Alice turned their heads, looking into the room to see Anna was sitting in her chair. She waved at them—a less than pleased look on her face. Then I slammed the door shut and made the door vanish again.

There was a moment of silence in the room before Alice looked over at me, "What do you have to do?"

"No!" Tasar shouted before pointing an accusatory finger at Alice. "I don't know who this is, but any plan involving some king of the veil and the person who tried to destroy the entire kingdom is one we should be running from, not encouraging!"

"The name's Alice," Alice stated, crossing her arms.

Tasar looked at her, nodding slightly, "My apologies. I am Tasar."

I stepped over to them, "I know you may not understand why I am doing this—"

"I get it," Alice cut me off, looking back over at me. "Tobyn said Kit died because he mattered to you. That is a type of guilt no person should have to live with. If you can do this and put the veil back before all hell breaks loose, I think you should do it."

"No! No, no, no, no," Tasar yelled. "Are you guys not understanding what you are saying? The veil was created because utter chaos was destroying our world!"

Alice sighed, looking at me, "I'm guessing you brought him here because he's smart?" Alice asked and I just nodded. She then looked over at Tasar, "Maisey is the princess of our kingdom, and her guilt isn't going to let her stop without trying to save him. If you are so smart, you should be able to help us get him back and get the veil back up without any problems. Plus, you want to tell the Queen you let her only child, heir to the throne, get herself killed?"

Tasar sighed, and I could physically see his willpower fall to the ground. I didn't know what he told himself that got him to agree, but he nodded at me. "Fine, I will help, but only because if you get yourself killed, I'll be sent to the gallows or worse...the stretcher," Tasar shuddered at the thought. "But we open it and, whether we have Kit or not, we close it before anything too bad gets through," Tasar stared at me.

I didn't want to agree with it, but I had to. I couldn't let my grief ruin everyone's lives again. "You're right," I agreed and Tasar sighed, putting his hands on his hips.

"So, what do we do?" Alice asked, and I let out a deep breath, walking over to one of Julianne's books. I flipped to a page and set it on the table in front of Tasar and Alice.

"From what I can tell, I have to make a symbol of time, wrapped in a circle of candles, that I will sit in after drinking the potion of endless time and worlds, chant the spell, and I should be transported into the world of knowledge."

Tasar nodded, a crease forming between his brows as he thought about what I said. Whatever he was thinking brought a silence over the room. "I have no idea what that means," Alice admitted, breaking the silence.

"That's why I'm here," Tasar said, pulling the book in front of him to read it himself.

Tasar worked on getting the spell ready while Alice and I just watched him. We tried to offer help, but he just made this grunting sound, motioning for us to back away from him. Alice and I stood by the small window, watching him make a large circle on the floor. He made eight circles, equal distances apart on the circle. He then connected each circle with the one across from it with a line. At the connection of all the lines was another circle and at the middle of the lines was another circle of dots. Every part of the circle was carefully put together and perfectly even. Then he left the room, after making us swear not to move, to get the potion together.

"I've never seen him so bossy," I said, looking over at Alice.

"It's nice seeing a man do all the work for once."

I nodded. "Why are you helping me?"

Alice paused, letting out a deep breath. She pursed her lips as she appeared lost in her own thoughts. "If I had the ability to bring back the people I lost, I would. No questions about it. No debate. I just…I can't sit here and pretend that I couldn't relate."

"Thank you."

"Doesn't mean this is a good idea."

I nodded, letting the silence take over the room again. Tasar came back after a half hour with a tall glass filled with a dark-brown liquid in one hand and a basket of candles in the other. "You're going to have to drink this," Tasar set the glass down in front of me.

I picked up the glass, moving it around, but the liquid barely moved at all. It was very thick and chunky, and when I sniffed it, a strong tangy smell burnt my nose. "I don't think I can keep that down," I said, shaking my head.

"If you want to save Kit, you don't have much of a choice."

I let out a deep breath, staring down at the glass. I have no choice. I reached around, plugging my nose and holding my head back to let the drink go down my throat. It was rotten and tangy and sweet with a hint of spoiled eggs. I gagged a total of three times before I finished.

Once the glass was empty, I pressed my mouth shut to keep everything inside and slammed the cup on the table. I was so close to keeping it down until I looked up at Alice, who was wincing with her hand over her mouth, and Tasar, who looked like he was watching a train crash. Then I instantly felt myself gag from the taste. I clasped my hands over my mouth, trying to take deep breaths.

Focus on your breathing, not the drink from hell.

Focus on your breathing, not the drink from hell.

. . .

AFTER I WAS PRETTY sure it was going to stay down, I lowered my hands. "What is next?" I asked quietly and Tasar nodded.

"I want you to sit in the center of the circle with your legs crossed, and Alice will hold the book up for you to read while I light the eight candles for each circle. You won't start until I light the first candle."

I followed his instructions, waiting for him to light the first candle. My legs were crossed with the backs of my hands resting on my knees as I did every morning during meditation. I stared at the pages, listening to the calmness of my heartbeat. A tingle ran from my toes slowly up my entire body. The words escaped my mouth in what I knew as the Neville native tongue. At first, my voice came out a little shaky, afraid of pronouncing some of the words wrong. Then my vision narrowed, everything around the words in front of me covered in a red fog. Then my words flowed from me like a language I had known my entire life. Eventually my eyes went black, and this sensation moved over me as if I wasn't part of my body anymore.

My legs were still crossed as I felt myself float above the ground. I watched everything around me, my eyes locking on my body sitting under me. Tasar walked over to Alice, putting a hand on her shoulder, and she lowered the book, holding it against her chest. A heat came off my hands, and I lifted them up, looking at the red glow pulsating around my fingers. I didn't know how I knew, but I lifted my hand higher, holding my palm facing away from me. With the right movement, my hand locked into place, pressure forming in the air around my hand. I lifted my other hand lower, and with the same movement I felt it too locked in place. Then with the shift of my hands in opposite directions

I was moving through different scenes, different languages, different realms. The more I moved the faster the realms changed, and the languages appeared as lines circling around me. I knew I shouldn't know them, but I didn't miss a single word or symbol. The more I saw, the more I knew.

The heat in my body started to rise, only getting hotter with each realm I passed. Suddenly the silence that shielded me like a cocoon was replaced with the rapid and heavy sound of my heart. My hands started to shake, the magic coming off my hand was getting brighter—so bright it was hard to look at. I tried to pull my hands back from the heat, but they weren't moving. The harder I pulled the faster everything seemed to move. A shooting pain ran through my head, and the only thing I could do was scream into the void.

In an instant, I was falling to the ground gasping for air, struggling to get everything to stop spinning. "Breathe Maisey. Just breathe." A familiar voice hit my ears, and I tried to move towards it, but I couldn't get myself up off the floor. I felt arms pull me up, and everything seemed to freeze. I stared at the dark-brown eyes looking back at me, the tan skin I remember touching, the long brown hair falling onto his broad shoulders instead of pulled back in a bun. "Just breathe," he said again. I felt tears in my eyes. His voice. It wasn't a ghost anymore. It was real. "In. Out. In. Out. Good job." He smiled slightly at me before his face started disappearing into the air around me, putting me back in my studio. Alice and Tasar stood on each side of me. The candles were all blown out, and the symbol underneath me was gone.

"Are you with us?" Tasar asked, turning my head to get me to look at him.

My body bent over, throwing up in the spot next to me. Once all the drink from hell had been expelled from my body, I started coughing, making it even harder to breathe. All I had to do was wait for myself to calm down. Once my body calmed down, I nodded, "Yeah, yeah, I'm here."

They helped me stand up, catching me when I stumbled.

"Did it work?" Alice asked, and I turned around, stumbling towards the table. I scrambled for the journal, flipping it open. There's only one way to find out. A white glow appeared behind the journal, and I could hear a soft voice talking back to me. A voice calling my name and begging me to listen. I leaned in, listening closer to the words. It was like a warning.

"What are you doing?" Alice asked and I looked up at her.

I placed my hand on the journal, and I could feel a heartbeat. The journal was alive now and ready to tell me all its secrets. The only thing I could hear was 'you can have everything you want,' and that was all I needed. "I have a plan," I whispered, a small smile spreading across my lips.

CHAPTER 8

The second I pulled myself from bed I was basically dragged into the closet. I didn't even get a second to look at the dress I was being forced into. The top corset part was dark red and with a diamond-encrusted Phoenix, and flared out towards the bottom, the color getting lighter the further down you went. It was fancier than my other dresses and tied even tighter. They slid my hands into long gloves that went up to my elbows, and they put diamonds on my wrists and around my neck. My hair was braided back and then I was ushered down the castle halls. It all moved so fast that I couldn't even ask what they were dressing me for or where I was going.

I just stayed silent as they walked me towards the main entrance of the castle. The double doors, crested with a Phoenix across it. From what I could tell, it was only used for special occasions—when whoever was entering or leaving wanted to make a scene.

Grace was standing behind the closed doors, waiting. She had to have been waiting for me because when she saw me, she motioned for me to stand next to her. "I wish you would wear your tiara at least," Grace said, and I sighed. "Just stand up straight, head held high, and smile."

"For who?" The doors started to open, and Grace put a soft smile on her face.

I quickly looked forward, straightening my back, and placing a matching smile on my face. Not enough to make my cheeks hurt, but enough to make sure whoever it was knew the smile was there. I stepped with her, keeping my pace as we walked down the stone walkway. A carriage pulled up, and we stopped, watching as the footman stepped off to open the door. I watched as a man dressed in dark blues and black, and a long cape strapped over his shoulders appeared. His hair was a thick black, holding his silver crown with blue crystals on his head. My body tensed as the blood left my face, examining the face in front of me. "He looks like him, but younger," I whispered, knowing my smile had long disappeared.

"He's your uncle, Heath. Your father's younger brother. He's king of Kisal."

Heath walked over to us, his green eyes lighting up as he looked at Grace, "Grace, my darling, looking as beautiful as ever." Grace held out her hands towards him, letting him place a kiss on the back of her hand. Grace took her hand back as soon as he moved away from it. I noticed her use her other hand to secretly wipe his kiss off. He looked back at me, staring at me differently than he did with Grace. Like he was surveying me. "Do princesses not wear crowns anymore?"

"They do. I don't. Thank you for coming all this way just to make that observation," I replied with the same judgmental tone he used. "Seeing how this is the first time we've met."

"My apologies. I did my uncle duties and brought gifts for

every birthday I missed. Enough to make up the time we have lost."

"Why don't we all go inside and talk?" Grace asked, intervening. "I have tea set up for us."

Heath nodded, walking with us as we headed towards the door, "I do hope you have something stronger."

"Her tea is stronger on its own," I stated, getting Heath to chuckle.

We walked into the main tearoom made strictly for guests. The room was made up of red walls, a nice light-brick fireplace, and a silver chandelier hanging from the ceiling. A brown table sat near the fireplace. Grace sat next to me at the table while Heath sat across from us. Servants brought in our tea and some sandwiches to go with it. "You're earlier than I expected," Grace said as soon as the door to the room closed.

"I thought it would be good for us to get to know each other before everyone shows up for the coronation," Heath answered, picking up two sandwiches. "How is the planning going? I do love myself a party."

"This is not a party. It is a celebration of the future of our kingdom. I expect all of us to be on our best behavior." She said 'all' but was only looking at Heath. "This is going to be an elegant gathering. I think our kingdom deserves it."

"You're right," I said, getting Grace to smile at me. "I know that I haven't always been a fan of this party—"

"Coronation, Maisey," Grace corrected, and I ignored her.

"But I know it's important to you, so consider me on board. I'm so on board that I even sent a list down of food I liked."

Grace smiled at me, reaching over to grip my hand.

"Speaking of the coronation," Heath said, getting our attention. "I was hoping we could discuss our future."

I could feel Grace's body tense, and her hand gripped mine a little tighter. "I'm not sure what you mean," Grace said, and Heath adjusted himself as well—straightening his back, clasping his hands in front of himself on the table.

"I'm just hoping to improve the relationship between our two kingdoms."

"Are you planning to need our relationship?" Grace asked, clearly referring to his intention to start a war. Professor Barter had discussed with me quite a few of the neighboring kingdoms, but Kisal was not one he went into detail about. Other than the brief mention of a tendency to go to war.

"If anyone decided to threaten our power, I think it's best people know we are united…as a family."

The second 'family' came out of his mouth, Grace stood up from the table, letting go of my hand. "I have items I must attend to. We will discuss this at a later date." She didn't wait for any agreement or for either of us to stand before she walked out of the room.

"You two are close," I stated, turning to look at Heath.

"Family is very complicated."

I sighed, looking down at my tea. I could understand it to a point, but I couldn't relate as strongly as I'm sure other people could. "It is of no point," Heath said. "Not anymore at least. Soon I will not need Grace's opinion, and something tells me that you and I have more in common in our leadership skills."

I opened my mouth to question him, but then I snapped it shut. Sometimes I found it best not to ask questions. Especially not when it was going to give me answers to questions I didn't want to know the answer to. We finished our tea in under ten minutes and much of it consisted of tense silence. I felt myself filtering my words the best I could without lying. I tried lying, and the way he looked at me…this wasn't a conversation. This was a test.

I walked out of the room, making my way through the castle and found Grace talking with the party planner in her personal tearoom. Normally they met in her office. She didn't hold meetings in her tearoom because it was the one place no one should have to worry about being bothered. "Can I have a word?" I asked, and when Grace nodded, the planner and her team let us be. I waited for the door to shut before looking at her. "You left pretty fast," I stated, and Grace sighed, walking over to sit on her white sofa. Her blush curtains were open, giving her full view of the kingdom in the distance.

"Your father loved your brother," Grace started to say, and her light-blue eyes glassed over in tears. "They were never too close, but as an older brother, it was his job to look out for Heath. I don't have a great relationship with my family, and theirs was much different than mine."

"What do you mean?"

"My father died when I was only four years of age. My mother got remarried after only a year. Not a surprise. Without a father, we had no money. We could barely survive. She was young and beautiful and with two daughters, she didn't have a choice. My stepfather was…just like my mother. They only cared about our family status, and the second Anna came of age, they pushed her towards marriage. The only time they found either of us useful was when it came to marriage."

"Anna made it seem like you were the favorite."

"I just didn't fight as hard as she did. They wanted me to get married to get status, and I wanted to get married to get out of the house. I just got lucky enough to find love behind it."

"That doesn't explain why things are so tense between you and Heath."

"Some people just don't mix well." Grace's tone didn't leave room for any more questions. As far as she was concerned, the conversation was over, but I wasn't done. She didn't have to talk to me. I've seen how information can travel through this castle. Information about me moved so fast, people didn't have to meet me to know some things about me.

So, I went to Professor Barter, who was always in there, back in the library in our normal working location. The second he saw me he went into lecture mode. Lecturing about the creation of the castle. The battle of a thousand deaths before peace was finally restored. I had a lot of problems with that, but I was mainly just waiting for the right moment to interrupt. It took me almost an hour before he stopped long enough to breathe and give me my chance. "You know, you've talked a lot about the other kingdoms," I stated, causing him to stop before he went into another long-winded speech.

"I do believe that is my job, as is this," Professor Barter used his slender pointer stick to tap against the board.

"You didn't talk much about Kisal, and that seems like something I should know about."

Professor Barter chuckled, moving to sit down across from me at the table, "I'm sure this conversation has a point to it."

"I want to know more about why you didn't talk about it."

"There's not much to say. It was conquered over twenty years ago, given to your uncle to look after, and they never tried to cause war." There was something stiff in his tone. Like things weren't as simple as he was trying to make them out to be.

"Just because they haven't caused war doesn't mean they are on our side."

He smiled, "You are a clever one."

"I'm not as adept in the roles of royal families, but I don't remember ever being told about a second son getting their own kingdom."

Professor Barter chuckled, "They don't. I believe it's a way to handle a situation when you have no other way to handle it."

I slightly nodded, "Handle the issue by getting it to go away on its own."

"I didn't say that."

"What do you mean? That sounds like it was exactly what you said."

"Look, I don't know what happened to make your grandfather decide this was the best thing for your father or uncle, but I do know that you don't assume why royalty does what they do." Again, it was another person not giving any room for future discussion. I think my people skills were getting worse; it had been so long since I'd had to sweet talk information out of someone—no, that wasn't entirely true. Sweet talk was never my thing. But outsmarting and semi-manipulating the conversation seemed to get me what I needed. Sounds worse than it was…maybe…I didn't know anymore.

Night was coming but sleep wasn't. Sleep was my enemy. It was like the bad storm that threatened to take everything away from you the second you let your guard down. I sat on my bed, covered by my long red robe with my legs crossed. My hair was down, laying over my tense shoulders. The moon was full in the night sky and the breeze was blowing my white curtains. "I should be honored you were actually waiting for me," I heard Odes' voice next to me. "Usually, I'm the one hunting you down."

"Hunting," I repeated his word, turning to look at him. He was standing at the side of his bed, dressed in his usual black and his hands clasped behind his back. "That's an interesting word choice."

"I don't come here to get a vocabulary lesson."

"You come here because you want something from me, and now I want something from you."

Odes slightly nodded, walking around my bed until he was standing at the foot of my bed, looking at me. "Last time I checked, you were getting something from me," Odes said with a small smirk appearing on his face.

I pressed my lips together, trying my best to control my irritation. "Don't test me."

"Don't test me," he snapped, and I hated myself for the slight jump that came from me. I didn't want to fear him and for the most part I didn't. He wasn't really here. From how he explained it, his power only let him project himself in the shadows of the moon. Yet, power radiated from him, just from his projection and I could feel the energy coming off him. What kind of power did he have on the other side?

"You know a lot," I stated, moving past the tension.

Odes nodded, letting the tension move as well.

"I want to know what you know about my father's brother."

"Why are you asking me? You have much better options."

"I try to talk to Anna as little as possible."

"That is not your only option," Odes unclasped his hands, bracing them on the end of my mattress. He leaned forward slightly, not breaking his eye contact with me. "You unlocked a part of yourself when you traveled realms. You don't need me to tell you what happened in the history of your family. You could see it."

"How did you know—"

Odes chuckled, straightening up, and pulled down at the ends of his sleeves, "As you said, I know a lot of things. You can find the answers on your own. You don't need me for that."

"Why can't you just tell me?"

"You won't learn if I do everything for you," Odes turned his back towards me, walking towards my window.

"You could just say you don't know," I stated, but if he heard, I wouldn't have known. He left before I could even finish my sentence. Proper goodbyes didn't seem to be his style. There were a lot of things that weren't his style. Some of which made him one giant red flag, but I wasn't ignoring it. No, but you are accepting it.

CHAPTER 9

I thought about using my powers to move through the past like Odes suggested, but I couldn't. I couldn't bring myself to see things that I wasn't supposed to see. Things I'm not supposed to know. The idea of violating King Lucius's privacy when he couldn't defend himself—there's nothing right in that. I couldn't guarantee what I was going to see or if I was going to understand it when I did, but it wasn't just my fear that worried me. It was the fear of seeing…intimate things. Even if I was able to run through his past, how could I control what I was able to see? I had enough scars in my past that I didn't need to add to them. I was going to be stuck doing things like I did when I thought magic was just an idea in books and stories. I was going to have to use my people skills. Do you have people skills?

I rolled my eyes at the question as I walked out of my bedroom and down the halls. I made it down the floor heading towards the library when I heard someone call my name. I stopped, turning around to see 'Uncle' Heath walking towards me from the other end of the hall. "Are you going to make me walk all the way over there?" he asked and I sighed, meeting him halfway. Heath spread his arms out towards me, looking at the new dress I was wearing. "You look beautiful. Light blue is a good color for you."

I looked at his arms, still raised. "I hope you aren't waiting for a hug," I stated, and Heath lowered his arms down to his sides.

"Normally women like me at first. They usually have to get to know me before they turn sour."

I looked at his smile, and there was this pit that filled my stomach. Like I was staring at dread itself. "Well, I guess I could get to know you."

"Perfect! Let's get to know each other," Heath walked over to stand next to me, holding his bent arm towards me. I held my breath, put my hand in the crook of his arm. He walked with confidence, but he also glanced around like he was watching for something—or watching out for someone. I wouldn't be surprised if a woman came out of nowhere to slap the hell out of him...

"Where are we going?" I asked.

"To the garden. It's a beautiful day, and I like to spend as much time as I can outside on a beautiful day."

My feet halted, getting him to stop with me. "W-why?" My eyes struggled to look at him, and there was a deep pounding in my chest. It had been a long time since I'd been there. Everything was moving so slow, and Kit was looking at me, needing me to save him.

I could feel eyes staring at me, and I looked over to see Heath with furrowed brows, "Why do I like beautiful days?"

"Why do you want to talk in the garden? On the castle grounds there are many places, tables, benches, a lake, a field to be outside in. Why the garden?"

Heath stared at me for a moment longer, like he was

reading words written all over my face. "Why don't you want to go to the garden?"

I felt my jaw clench at his question. He was asking, but the cockiness of his eyes said that he already had an idea. I knew what was waiting at the garden, and I didn't want Heath to be there. He didn't deserve to be there…but I couldn't stop him. Not without doing something I would regret. I didn't want to be stuck trying to explain this to a man who hadn't even talked to his brother for who knows how long or else he would have been here when we burned his body under the stars. Grace said the stars were all the Gods' eyes welcoming him to a better place. All of that and his brother, who I didn't even know existed, was nowhere to be found.

I pushed down the nerves burning in my chest. "Let's go," I suggested, letting us continue to walk down the halls toward the exit.

I held my breath the closer we got to the garden. The first thing I saw was the wooden arch, carefully carved with flowers and vines moving up the sides. At the top of the arch was a carving of a God. A God of garden or flowers or something. I couldn't keep track.

Heath stopped at the white rose bushes just around the entrance. He held a flower between his two fingers. "I wonder how they are able to keep the flowers going this well."

"Cordelia does it. She's lead—"

"Fairy, I know." He dropped the flower from his hand, annoyance flashing over his face. He looked at me, sighing. "She doesn't like me."

A laugh broke through my lips, "Somehow that doesn't surprise me."

"Some people are just threatened by us."

"Because we wear crowns?" I asked, looking around. We

were in the section of roses. Kit's ashes weren't with the roses, but I could feel him watching me.

"No, because we see the truth of the world," Heath dropped my arm to sit on the stone bench near us. "Think about it, Maisey. You had nothing. Just one drop of blood and all of this would be yours just when the kingdom's future was on the line."

"What are you talking about?" I asked, looking at him.

"No one believed you were going to come back. I had many meetings for my brother, pushing back the annulment of your crown."

"Annulment?"

"They wanted to dissolve your throne and your power. Then they would unite our kingdoms under my rule."

"And you're telling me this, so I—what? Revel in your generosity?"

"I tell you this to educate you. People will always be after us. The power we hold, the insight others fail to see. It scares them." Every word he said was calculated, I knew this. Yet, I could feel a part of myself falling for it. Falling for the words he didn't say, the words left floating in-between the lines.

I forced a fake scoff, shaking my head. "I don't see our similarities. People were happy to see me when I arrived." My memory quickly jumped to Anna trying to kill me the first time she saw me. "Well, all but one."

Heath chuckled. "I always liked Anna, she was a wild one. As for everyone else, I will admit that some things were less than ideal when I left my home. But your mother is just scared of the indulgences she wishes to fulfill when I'm around. Can't fault my brother for worrying."

My head snapped towards him. "What is that supposed to mean?"

"My brother has always been cautious." Heath looked at

me with a smirk. "Something tells me that you are not like that."

"Are you suggesting you and Grace had a relationship?"

Heath smiled at me. "You look like me." Before I could say anything more, a woman dressed in his castle colors of dark blues and black walked towards us, calling his attention. Heath nodded, standing up from the bench. He gave me one last look. "Looks like I'm needed. We should talk more later." I watched him walk out of the garden, and I was left with a foreign feeling running through me.

Heath was up to something. I knew that. Why was my mind refusing to accept that he was a liar? Why wouldn't he be a liar? I knew the best way to cause chaos was with lies that mess with people's heads. It was how Anna got all her power when she wasn't physically destroying people's lives.

"My brother has always been cautious. Something tells me that you are not like that."

"You look like me."

No. It couldn't be. He's a liar. I couldn't let him get to me. If I let every liar get in my head, I would amount to nothing. I was here to get Kit back. That was the reason that I stayed. I could have found my way back to my small apartment, working in the diner until my magic finally killed me. I would be alone, but I wouldn't be crushed under the weight of responsibility. Everywhere I turned there was something waiting to take me down. I would not let him get the chance. I would prove he was a liar, and then I would throw him out.

I picked up the ends of my dress to move quicker as I ran back into the castle and down the hall. I found my familiar path to Tasar's office, but this time I didn't find the need to knock. Apparently, I came in too loud because he jumped, falling off his chair, and since his legs were hiked up on the desk, he hit the floor hard. I think I heard a book he was holding hit his face. Tasar let out a stream of curses before standing up and looking at me from over his desk. "Maisey, I have grown rather fond of you, more than most people, but do you always have to come in here with full force?"

"I usually knock."

Tasar huffed, pushing himself up with the table. "Even when you knock, you are in a hurry and knock a painting off the wall."

"Well, do a better job of nailing them down. I have an emergency!" I shut the door, walking deeper into his office. "I need to know if there is a way to test my blood to the late King."

"Why would you want to do that?"

"I need it to prove a point."

Tasar paused for a moment just staring at me. Then he nodded slightly. If there was a conversation going on, it was all in his head. "Listen, I don't know who said what, but there is no point in testing anything. Both the queen and the king accepted you and named you their heir. Because the King is no longer alive, they can't contest his will. Your rule is quite literally set in stone."

I crossed my arms over my chest. "Why would you say that?"

"What do you mean?"

"I know why I am asking what I am asking, but how could you know why I am asking what I am asking, unless there is a valid rumor going around this castle that is exactly what I am asking."

Tasar sighed. "There are many rumors in this castle that you don't know."

"So, there is a rumor!"

"It's the same rumor that has surrounded this castle since your uncle was kicked out. Rumors that I will not tell you. If you want to know them, you can ask the Queen."

"And if I command you to tell me?"

Tasar scoffed, crossing his arms. "You could and I will deny. You can have me arrested and I will deny. The Queen will find out, and she will let me go. Then I will be mad at you, and you will feel guilty for locking up a friend that knows about your dirty little secret in your so-called art studio."

"Hey! There is art in there! And I'll have you know, Grace weirdly loves them all!"

"She's your mother. I heard it's what they do."

I sighed, letting my arms fall back down to my sides. There was something about the way he said 'heard' that settled in me. It's not like I would know. Things I had made, even when I had given them to my most recent foster family, most of them didn't really care. I guess I should thank her for that.

ONE THING I liked about being in the castle, it usually only took me asking one person to find who I was looking for. Grace was in the dining hall of the castle with two long tables full of different, very decorated cakes. A pink one, a white one, a chocolate one, a yellow one, and so on. With every big cake, there were two small plates in front of them with slices for tasting. Grace was on one side, examining the cakes while two other women, one middle aged and the other in her teens, were on the other. They must have heard me because they all looked over, a smile spreading across Grace's face. "Maisey, perfect!" she cheered, ushering me forward. She loved planning this party. I could tell every time I saw her handling a part of it. "Come look at the different cakes. I know you told me to pick because you will like any, but I would like to at least have you taste a few." I stood next to Grace, smiling at the two women. "Mrs. Markson is the best cake creator in the whole kingdom, and her daughter is learning the trade." The girl's face lit up when Grace spoke to her. Her mother was being praised by the Queen, hard not to have pride in that. "Every cake has a little bit of magic."

"I just make them. They find their own power in their taste." Mrs. Markson said.

I slightly nodded, looking over at Grace. "I would like to speak with you."

Grace nodded, looking at Mrs. Markson and her daughter. "Leave us, please."

They nodded and I thanked them as I watched them walk towards the door. Grace looked back at the cakes, picking up one of the slices in front of the white cake with gold dots. "Try this."

She handed me the plate. The inside of the cake had three layers with a slightly brown tint. I took a bite of the cake. It was fluffy and smooth. The icing was very sweet and once I swallowed, I tasted nuts. I looked over at Grace, who was watching me carefully. "Very good, but not a fan of the strong nut aftertaste," I said, setting the plate on the table, and Grace smiled a bittersweet smile at me.

"Your father didn't like nuts either." She looked away, her mind clearly drifting to fond memories.

"I have to ask you something," I said and Grace nodded, looking at the cakes again. "I want to know why Heath had to leave the castle."

Grace shook her head. "Nothing you must worry yourself with."

"You know, there are rumors in the castle."

"There are always rumors." Grace picked up a plate with a pink slice of cake in front of the cake with pink and red flowers styled on it. "Try this one."

I took a bite of the cake. The strawberry taste was strong and not as sweet as the nut one. "I like strawberries, especially in ice cream, but not really in frosting," I said setting the plate down next to the other. "I just want to know why there is so much tension. I know there is a secret that you are keeping from me."

Grace pointed at the white cake. "I think this is too plain."

I nodded, trying to keep my frustrations from boiling over. I couldn't be distracted by cakes. Especially for a party that I didn't care to have in the first place. "I like the colorful ones. Now, will you please talk to me?"

Grace sighed, finally turning to give me her full attention. "The secret has nothing to do with you. Heath has always been one that likes to conquer his desires, and there are some that he will never get. Certain events made it clear that his behavior couldn't continue in this castle. Especially not when I found out we were having a girl. I wanted to make sure you didn't see the way your uncle used women, and the servants we had to replace after they thought he was in love." Grace may not have meant for me to see her roll her eyes when she turned, but I still caught it. "He never lied to them, but he knew what to do to make them lie to themselves. He played on that." She reached over for the yellow and green frosted cake, handing another plate to me. "Try the lemon. I love lemons."

I slipped a bite into my mouth. The sweetness was strong, and the lemon in the cake was a nice balance. "The best, so far," I said, setting the plate down. Grace smiled, placing a toothpick I didn't even realize she was holding into the lemon cake. I thought about turning and leaving the room before she handed me another plate, but my feet didn't move. My feet didn't move, but my mouth did before I could even think about it. "There is another thing I wanted to discuss with you."

"And what is that?" Grace looked back at me, and I felt my hands nervously playing with the skirt of my dress.

I shouldn't be bringing this up. She didn't need to hear it, and I didn't know why I wanted to say it. I took a deep breath in, looking back at the cakes at the table to avoid her gaze. "I was talking to someone, and I realized how you keep my art. Even the bad ones. No one has ever kept something I created. I want to say thank you."

"Don't thank me for being your mother," Grace said, and I looked up to see a soft smile on her face. "Speaking of which, I have assigned a guard to be stationed outside your door."

That shot my nerves on fire. Not being able to leave my room without a guard keeping track of where I was going? No, thank you. "Why?"

"Because it's customary when there is a guest. Any guest."

I bit the inside of my cheek, keeping my mouth shut. I reached over, picking up a piece of the chocolate cake. I took a bite, trying not to focus on Grace smiling at me. The chocolate was smooth and so…chocolate. "This chocolate one is good!" I smiled, looking back at Grace.

By the time I made it back to my bedroom, the guard was already standing there. He bowed his head as I walked past him, and into my bedroom. I didn't like the idea of him being out there. It made it that much harder to leave unnoticed. Now, I was trapped in my room, pacing across the red rug in the center. I can't bring Kit back, if I can't get out of my bedroom! One of the mirrors in my room cracked at a sudden burst of rage and I groaned. This was all his fault. He showed up and now I was being watched. I didn't have to be watched before. I could handle my business without having to be seen. When I heard another crack on a different mirror, I knew I had to do something. I walked over to my desk, grabbing a piece of paper I had sitting on my desk. It's time for him to leave.

. . .

DEAR UNCLE HEATH,

Ever since our talk in the garden, I started to think things over. I was paranoid about what you meant between every word you said, and then I realized you were manipulating me. You were twisting words and trying to get in my head. I started to question things that shouldn't be questioned. Bending the honor of people that can't defend themselves. I don't know why you came to this castle or what you wished to accomplish or doubt you wanted to plant. It's not going to work. Consider this your sign to stop whatever you're planning, pack up your belongings, and get the hell out of my kingdom. Consider this me saying it nicely because I will not do it again.

--Princess Maisey

MY ENTIRE BODY was raging to the point that my hands were shaking. When I signed 'Princess' I was asserting every ounce of power I was told I had. If it didn't work…I felt like I could destroy the castle just to get rid of him. Red flashed through my eyes and the corners of the letter started to burn. I cursed, blowing out the flames. The damage stuck to the white edges of the paper. If this didn't get him out, he had a death wish.

I folded the letter, standing from my desk, and walking towards my bedroom door. I swung open the door, looking around to see a knight standing by the windows. I cleared my throat, and the knight quickly looked over at me. He slightly bowed his head again.

"Give this to my uncle," I said, handing him the letter.

"You put it in his hand, and you tell him that I meant it from the bottom of my heart." The knight nodded, walking down the hall. I turned back into my bedroom the second he turned the corner. All that was left was to wait. He would be gone. He had to be.

CHAPTER 10

I was interrupted from my morning meditation by being called to the throne room as soon as possible. I learned soon after starting daily meditation that I didn't handle missing them very well. It was the closest I could get to sleep without drowning in my regret. I changed as fast as I could with a frown plastered on my face. I ran a brush through my hair before walking out of my room. The guard was still standing by my door just as he was when I entered. He didn't say anything. He just bowed his head as I walked past. All I could hear was the sound of my shoes on the floor. The halls were emptier than normal. It felt as if everyone was hiding from me. I could have thought I was being paranoid, but then the door to the throne room swung open as I got close to it, though no one was there that could have opened them.

The throne room was large enough to fit the normal number of people in the castle and guests for a party when we had them. It was beautifully designed with reds and whites, except for the marble floor. On the floor was the depiction of what everyone recognized as the Great War.

The war that made Neville a kingdom in the first place. Grace was sitting on one of the large stone thrones. They were beautiful, stained black to represent the ashes the kingdom rose from. Heath stood near her; his hand placed firmly on his hips. A word wasn't said until the doors to the room closed. At least I didn't close them. "Maisey, your uncle claimed that you wrote him a letter demanding that he leave." Grace spoke with nothing but annoyance.

"Clearly it didn't work since he's still here," I stated, getting a glare from Heath.

"You have no right to force me out of the castle!" Heath shouted.

"I believe I do. I am reigning princess, heir to the throne, and the first born of King Lucius," Thank you history books! "I believe that is exactly my right."

Heath glared at me. "You—"

"Heath!" Grace snapped, getting him to look away from me. "I am willing to sort this situation out. Let's not say anything that is going to make this worse."

Heath nodded, his jaw clenching. "I don't know what I would have done to upset you," he said to me, but the anger he held in his eyes said differently. "We are family. We should be able to talk it out."

You came here to destroy the fabric of this castle for some twisted desire for Grace and the kingdom. You are going to be gone within the hour or I'm going to force you out. You stay away from me, and I won't kill you.

That was what I wanted to say. I doubted he would call my bluff, and, if we were alone, I probably would have said it. If we were alone, and he had decided to tell Grace, it would have been his word against mine. She didn't even like being in the room with him, but it was hard to blindly agree with someone when you were there to see exactly what happened.

I held my breath, clasping my hands together in front of me. I'm just an emotional Princess who let her emotions get the best of her. I looked up at Grace. "Grace, may Heath and I have a moment of privacy? I'm sure we can work this out like adults."

She paused for a moment, debating before looking at Heath. He nodded, and Grace looked back at me. She let out a deep breath, nodding her head as well as standing up from the throne. "I hope you two work this out, guards will be outside to notify me of any yelling," she stated, giving my arm a supportive squeeze as she walked past me. I watched her walk through the door, and the guards shut them behind her.

My entire body shifted the second we were alone. I looked back at Heath with a tilt of my head. "Are you done pretending you don't understand why I sent that letter?"

Heath glared at me. "Looks like I'm not the only one going around pretending."

"I sent that letter as a form of peace."

"You call a threatening letter at night a sign of peace?"

"It's better than just having the guards throw you out of the castle."

Heath stared at me for a moment before breaking his hard gaze with a scoff. He looked away from me, shaking his head as a slight chuckle left his lips. "Let's be honest for a moment." Heath walked over to sit on the steps in front of the throne. He looked up at me with a smirk on his face. "We both know I said what I did to get to you. I wanted to know what you would do. I even did it near the body of the man who died for you. I figured it would make you vulnerable enough to let your guard down."

"Why would you do that?"

"I wanted to know what you would do. I heard stories about you. A young princess raised in a world of no magic, no family, no ties. The princess that was thrown back into this world. The number of bodies that followed you. Do you still hear them scream as you sleep? If you're sleeping."

I swallowed hard, staring at him. "How do you know that?" My voice came out quiet.

"Lucius and I weren't gifted with magic, but anyone can learn parlor tricks. Like following the magic trail of someone. It's like holding onto a string throughout a kingdom. You follow it and play through the scenes that hold the most magic. It's like watching a play unfold. You don't miss a single thing."

"Is there a point to this?"

"I don't know what you are up to. I don't know what you have planned. Why you would decide to stay after you lost so much." Heath pushed himself back up, walking towards me. "You want to know what I think?" I didn't say anything, but I didn't have to. "You have a plan to fix things, and when it all blows up in your face, I will be there to take everything away from you. Maybe then the next time you want to send a little letter asserting your power, you'll be queen enough to show some power." I felt my eyes flash red and he chuckled again.

He walked past me, heading towards the exit. I balled my fist, hearing the doors open and shut. My magic boiled inside of me. It wanted to rip his head off, tear off his arms, and throw him off the cliff. He though he was so smart. Like he knew something! He didn't know anything! Like I was destined to destroy everything! I was helping everyone! I was fixing the mistakes that let Anna run everything and everyone into the ground!

I heard the harsh sound of stone cracking, feeling a shift under me. I looked around to see a crack form at the center of the battle working its way towards me. I quickly shook my head, taking a deep breath in. No, no, no, no! I really can't answer questions about how a crack got into the floor! The more I focused on it, the faster it seemed to move. I quickly moved back like it was a snake trying to sink its fangs into me.

The door opened and my entire body froze. I looked over at the doors to see Beatrice walk into the room. I let out a deep breath, looking down at the crack unable to find it again. "The Queen wanted me to check on you while she had people assist your uncle as he left," Beatrice explained, and I looked over at her.

"I'm fine," I said, letting out a deep breath and making my way towards the exit.

"I hate to speak out of turn, but I can tell something is plaguing your heart," Beatrice said and I stopped, looking at her. "And I don't think it had anything to do with your uncle."

"What do you think it is?"

"The same thing that plagues us all. Losing someone we love, and you've lost three. I know you didn't know your father and Anna wasn't a joy to be around, but we all have expectations of what our family is supposed to be like. Death isn't always a bad thing."

"How is dying when you aren't supposed to not a bad thing?"

"Death is natural. Sometimes it is what happens by someone else's action, but it is natural nonetheless. It's a way for us to fix our past mistakes."

This cold chill ran through my body. Something was wrong. My eyes narrowed at her. "Who have you been talking to?" I asked.

Beatrice sighed, "That's not important. They have helped me see that everything happens for a reason, and Kit knew that better than anyone. He believed that magic was supposed to help people, not avoid a way of life. We are born, we try to survive, and then we die. It's the way it works."

"He didn't know he was going to die like that! Being linked to a monster, having his heart squeezed, and falling from a tree!"

"In life we have choices. It was war, and he made a choice to stay with you. Pastor Gregory says that we must live by our actions!" Beatrice quickly pressed her lips together. Pastor Gregory. I knew I should have…

"I have work to do." I spoke softly and Beatrice quickly nodded before walking out of the room.

KIT KNEW BETTER THAN ANYONE.

He believed that magic was supposed to help people, not avoid a way of life.

We are born, we try to survive, and then we die.

He didn't want to die.

He didn't plan to die.

He wasn't supposed to die.

WATER FILLED MY EYES, and I held my breath, hoping to keep every dark feeling raging inside from exploding into every part of this castle. I could shatter everything around me. The weight of the entire day was trying to crush everything inside of me. A single tear fell down my cheek and I clenched my jaw as sobs broke through all my barriers. I covered my mouth, hoping no one would hear me as I turned away from the door. I looked at the thrones, the vision of them blurring. Every drop of blood that came from my hands flashed through my eyes. Every piece of anger wanted to spill out of me. My hands started to shake and no matter how hard I tried they wouldn't stop. A large pit formed in the bottom of my stomach and the air around me seemed to evaporate. I put my hand on my heart, feeling my body start to cave into the floor under me. Then two hands touched my arm, and I looked up, trying to focus on them.

"Maisey, you must breathe." I could hear Alice's voice, but I couldn't seem to get the tears to clear enough for me to see her. "If you don't breathe you are going to bring this entire castle to the ground."

In and out. In and out. In and out. In and out. In and out.

The longer I focused on my breathing the less pounding there was in my ears. The less my hands shook. I quickly wiped my eyes and the stream of tears off my cheeks. I was now able to make out Alice's face. She rubbed my arms, giving me a reassuring smile. "The whole castle started to shake. I saw some servants drop to their knees in fear."

"I'm sorry," I choked out, trying to clear up my face the best I could.

"You don't have to apologize. Maisey, if you don't let someone in, you're going to crush under the pressure."

I didn't have the energy to argue. I didn't have time. "We aren't doing this now. Later tonight we are going to meet in my studio. Tell Tasar to be there as soon as the sun sets. We're getting Kit back."

Alice nodded, forcing back any other concerns she had before walking out of the throne room. I looked back down at the battle pictured under my feet. The battle with blood, anger, and fear created this kingdom around me. They used what they needed to get what they wanted, and people honored them for it. We toast them on the anniversary. We tell stories about them. I wasn't doing anything wrong. I was doing what I need to do to make things right!

CHAPTER 11

Since Heath had left the castle, the guard didn't have to wait outside my bedroom. I had a feeling he was just as happy about this as I was, but I didn't think he was as open to showing it as I was. By the time night came around, I was already in my studio. I waited for a knock, and when it finally came, I walked over to unlock the door. The second I swung open the door, I felt my entire body tense. Beatrice was standing on the other side of the door, holding some papers close to her chest. "I'm sorry to interrupt," Beatrice said lightly, smiling at me.

I held my breath, trying to push down the nerves swirling inside of me. "What are you doing up here?"

"I just want to give you something. I think it's going to help with what we talked about earlier." She handed the papers over to me and I nodded slightly. "Goodnight." She turned around, walking away, and I shut the door.

I didn't bother looking at the papers before tossing them onto one of the tables. I had no interest in the conversation nor what she was trying to get me to read. What did pique my interest was the journal.

It seemed to pulse the second I stepped in front of it. It glowed like breaths being taken. I could hear its whispers calling. It wanted to be used. It wanted me to use it to make things right. It understood what I wanted and what I needed.

The door swung open, and I lifted my hands, about to hurt whoever it was. "Whoa, whoa, whoa!" Tasar yelled as I lowered my hand. "Watch where you point those things!"

Alice pushed past him, rolling her eyes as she walked deeper into the room. Tasar shut the door, and they both stood by the table in front of me. "Have you found anything else out?" Alice asked and I looked down at the pages around me.

The words pulsated in front of me as my eyes struggled to keep them in focus. My fingers slid across the pages, slowly making my way to the page of the spell. A heat came off the page as the words threatened to come for me. "Maisey." I heard Alice's voice as I tightly squeezed my eyes closed. "What do you need us to do?"

I looked back at the words, forcing myself to go back to the pounding and brightness. Reading along the pages until some bolded on the page. The book was caving to my needs.

THE SEALS **open from others with matching power of the first witch.**

A single vial of the first marked.

The heart of the uncorrupted in a world filled with torment.

The sword crafted from the souls of the innocent in the core of the Kingdom.

Under the red moon in the site of creation is the seal of those lost.

. . .

A PAIN STABBED through my mind, getting me to close my eyes again. I could hear the book slam shut as I pressed my fingers against my head. "Anything?" Tasar asked, getting me to pry my eyes open to them watching with concern.

"Um, I was able to read what we needed, but understanding how to get it, not so much."

"What do we need?" Alice asked and I let out a deep breath, lowering my hand from my head as the pain very slowly became bearable.

"The seals come from others with power that matches the first witch." I said, looking at Tasar.

"I think that means you," he said.

Me. The idea should have made me feel better. I didn't have to convince someone else that this was a good idea…or be told how bad of an idea it was.

"What else?" Alice asked, pulling me out of my head.

"A single vial of the first marked."

"My guess—the blood of the first marked is the reason for the veil in the first place, but I'll have to look in the history books." Tasar stated.

"I'll do that," I quickly said. Odes has to know where I can get that. If not, he was completely useless. "We need the heart of the uncorrupted in a world filled with torment."

"A unicorn!" Alice shouted. "Sorry, I got excited. I actually know this one."

"Unicorn?" I asked. "And I thought nothing could surprise me anymore."

"Unicorns don't exist," Tasar stated, rolling his eyes. "They were wiped out for the power of their horns."

"They were almost wiped out. It's believed that there are still five that survived. They never change into their true forms, never breed, and because unicorns never die, they are still around," Alice explained.

"Who told you that?" Tasar's voice was soaked with disbelief and slight irritation.

"I was told a lot of things at my old job."

"Just because you were told that, doesn't make it true."

Alice scoffed, crossing her arms. "Okay, if it's not a unicorn, what is it?"

Tasar paused, clenching his jaw as he glared at her.

"Okay, well, we have to find one first," I stated. And rip its heart out, I thought, seeming to be the only one affected by that notion. "Alice, how about you work on finding a unicorn, hopefully a bad one."

She smirked at Tasar. "Happily."

"Lastly, we need the sword crafted from the souls of the innocent?" It sounded fake as it came out of my mouth. It didn't help that I ended up getting them both to look at me in confusion.

"I'm lost again," Alice mumbled, shaking her head.

"Tasar?" I looked at him, and his face went blank.

His eyes were looking right through me, his lips parted, slightly twitching as he tried to speak.

"I think I see smoking coming out of his ears," Alice whispered towards me, like he wasn't standing right next to us.

"I have no idea," Tasar said, finally looking at us. "And I know a lot."

"Oh, oh, oh! Maybe the sword was used for executions!" Alice exclaimed.

"It says souls of the innocent," Tasar stated.

"Are you saying all of those people are guilty?"

"I'm saying they aren't all innocent!"

"Okay!" I yelled, getting them both to look back at me. "It says a weapon created from innocent souls. There has to be a book talking about how weapons are created."

"You would have to talk to the weaponsmith," Tasar said,

not even trying to hide the dread in his voice. "And I say you because I'm not doing it."

Alice shrugged, a sly smirk on her face. "I could do it."

"Yeah, that won't work," Tasar stated, making her smirk disappear.

"I will do it," I stated, letting out a deep breath.

"Okay, so what is the man that knows everything going to do?" Alice asked, her own judgment in her voice.

"It said, under the red moon in the site of creation is the seal of those lost." I explained, looking at Tasar. "You have to try to find that."

Alice scoffed. "Glad I got unicorns."

I let out a deep breath, looking down at the book in front of me. "We will get all the things, I will translate the spell, and learn how to get it closed after we get Kit back."

"And we better move fast," Tasar pointed out, making my head snap up towards him. "The red moon is going to be here in two weeks, that's if it's on time. It's rare and inconsistent. If we aren't ready by then, I don't think we'll get another chance."

Don't panic. Don't panic. "Looks like we have work to do."

* * *

ONCE I WAS ALONE AGAIN, there was only one thing that I needed to think about. Sadly, there was only one person I needed to talk to. I hate reading, but there was no other choice to be made. I was the one who needed him, and he liked me to know it. I was sitting in the center of the room with my legs crossed, my eyes closed, and the book closed in front of me. A chill traveled through my spine and as he appeared behind me, a breeze coming from nowhere sent tingles up my arms. "You know what you need now," Odes commented in the silence. I didn't say anything until he walked around me, stopping once he was in front of me.

"I need a vial of the first marked," I stated, looking up at him.

"Anna knows where it is but get it last. No point of wasting it if you fail."

"Is that lack of faith I am hearing?"

"For someone who is supposed to have so much to gain, you are taking longer than I expected. Does make me start to think if I should be questioning your commitment to your hunter friend."

I shot up from my spot on the floor, glaring at him. "Watch what you say to me."

"I mean no insults."

"You could have fooled me."

"I'm just suggesting that we focus on what we are working for." Odes lifted his hand, another breeze coming, but this one was accompanied by the sound of pages turning. I looked down at the glowing book between our feet. It glowed brighter, showing me another spell to look at. I felt myself being called towards the glow, lowering myself back onto the floor. The words danced around the page, begging for me to call their name. My fingers touched the softness of the page, giving it exactly what it asked for. I chanted every word feeling a warmth, a power, travel from my fingers, up my arms straight to my eyes. I was embraced by a bright red light, pulling me away from this world and lifting me into another.

THEN I WAS STANDING ONCE AGAIN, another breeze causing me to open my eyes. I was in the middle of a forest, trees so tall I could barely see their tops. Everything around me was tinted in darkness. The sky was gray, the grass was a burnt yellow. Then I noticed the tall figure standing with its back toward me. The broadness of his shoulders and strength in his arms…brown hair pulled back in a bun and tattoos moving up his arms to the ends of his black shirtsleeves. "K-Kit." My voice cracked, and I watched him slowly turn around, aiming his arrow straight towards me.

"I'm not falling for this again," he stated, releasing an arrow before I could say another word. My breath hitched in my throat, noticing how his eyes grew wide. I looked down, noticing the lack of an arrow in my stomach. I glanced over my shoulder to see the arrow lodged into the tree directly behind me. "How are you here?" Kit asked, getting me to look back at him.

"I found a book. It's filled with spells. I-I…" So much of what I wanted to tell him wanted to come out all at once, but I didn't know how much time I had. "I-I am so happy to see you." I stepped closer to him. He was so close to me, but it was like he wasn't there at all. There was this glass between us, keeping me from feeling him again.

"I don't remember much about what happened," Kit said, quickly looking around. "I can't stay in one place for long."

"I'm going to fix this."

"Maisey," Kit reached up, coming so close to my cheek, but not actually touching my skin. "You can—"

THEN HE WAS GONE. I was thrown on the hard floor, gasping for breath as my eyes shifted back to the wood of my studio. Tears brimmed in my eyes and I quickly closed them before any could make it down my cheeks. Everything was taken out of me. All I could do was lay there in my own pain.

* * *

I WAS SUPPOSED to be meeting with Grace for afternoon tea, and she made it very clear she would be very unhappy if I missed it. I did wonder what she would do, but a part of me was scared to find out. When I walked into her tearoom, I expected it to be like every other time. I was wrong. Not only were there other people, but rows of different dresses were lined up against the wall. In the center of the room was a round, wooden box with mirrors on three sides. This was a dress fitting. I tried to turn on my heels and escape the trap, but the large door was shut by the guards outside, and Grace had her arm linked with mine before I could stop her. "This is going to be so much fun!" Grace told me, and I scowled at her.

"You tricked me."

"I know you want me to just plan everything, but I can't guess your measurements." She pulled me towards the four-woman set to measure and dress me like a doll. "This will be over in no time."

Not only did Grace trick me, but she was also a liar. This was not fun. I started losing track of the number of dresses I was being forced into behind the divider. Red dresses, white dresses, gold dresses; V-neck, turtle neck, sweetheart neck; long sleeves, short sleeves, cap sleeves; dresses that needed my hair up, dresses that needed my hair down; jewels, no jewels; short train, long train, extra-long train. I could feel myself getting dizzy watching the three women race around me like mice looking for cheese. I didn't even remember if I made any choices or what the final dress was going to look like.

The only thing I did know when I walked out of the room was that my head hurt, and my body was as heavy as stone. I stopped halfway down the hall, leaning against the wall. I didn't even care that people were watching me. They didn't have to be shoved into different dresses for hours. They didn't even have any food! Even though, I doubt they would have let me touch it if they did.

My eyelids started to get heavy, threatening to close. "Princess?" I quickly jumped at the strange voice, turning around. I recognized his face from when he was forced to stand outside my bedroom. "Would you like to me to call upon a servant to help you get some rest?"

"I'm not tired." You were just lying on the wall.

"Pardon me for this, Princess, but I've noticed sleep hasn't been accompanying you most nights."

"Why would you say that?"

"I could hear you in your chambers pacing when I was in charge of watching over you, plus, I am on night watch most nights. I've seen you roaming the halls." I think he saw the quick glance of worry on my face as he said, "I did not say a word. It is not my place."

"Good. I am fine," I claimed again before just walking away from him before another word could be said. Sleep was for those who were able to save someone they cared about. Sleep was for someone who had what they needed, someone who translated the spell, someone who knew what they had to do and did it. I needed to get there. The red moon was coming, and I would be ready for it.

CHAPTER 12

The castle weaponsmith station was towards the back of the castle down a floor with its own little section. The large metal doors were shut, and all I could hear were a string of curse words and metal clanking. I asked around about this place, and I was met with worried looks and wide eyes. I was even told not to go down there if I wanted to keep knowing what happiness was like. The idea of opening the door with a sign that said 'Fuck Off' was terrifying. I pushed the door, meeting nothing but resistance. It's locked.

I knocked and the cursing stopped, but no one opened the door. I knocked again, and there was nothing but silence. So, I went back to Maisey Collins, orphaned and living in foster homes. I took my fists and pounded on the door with speed and force that no person with ears could ignore. "Alright!" a voice yelled, but I didn't stop. "Stop!" I didn't stop. Then I heard the door unlock and swing open, hitting me with this intense heat and the strong smell of sweat.

An old man opened the door. He was half my height, full white hair, and his skin was golden with dark spots and wrinkles. His eyes were black, and his frown was heavy. "What the hell is wrong with you?"

"What the hell is wrong with you? Not only do you lock the door, but you act like you don't hear me knock."

"I'm old, I got bad ears."

"How would you know to stop cursing and be as quiet as a mouse, if you had bad ears?"

The old man paused for a moment. "I don't know what you are talking about." He just huffed, scurrying back into the workroom and I followed him, much to his dismay. "Why are you bothering me?"

"I need information on a weapon, and I was told you would know it."

"What idiot told you that?"

"If I needed you to know that I would tell you," I stated, hearing him cuss at a few things as he walked to his station. The whole place was cluttered with tools, metals, tables, and scraps. I didn't know what half the things did, but how he found his way around amazed me. He moved like he lived in this room all his life. He moved around, weaved through all the clutter without hitting a thing. While I was tripping over pieces of metal, bumping into tables, knocking down tools.

"What do you need to know, so I can get you the hell out of here?" the old man asked, and I sighed, using the sleeve of my dress to wipe off the sweat accumulating on my forehead.

"I need to know about a really old sword, and where to find it."

"Have you not been into the armory?"

I nodded, remembering the first time I stepped inside the weapons room. "I have."

The weapons room was giant and filled with every type of weapon. Different sized swords, axes, large hammers, even a large, curved knife gathered on the walls. Throwing stars, arrows, and different knives lay on the table. That was only the few things I could recognize, but it certainly wasn't all of it.

"Did you make every weapon in there?" I asked.

"Every single one. Every day. Every hour. Every minute." The old man had a smile on his face. Then he noticed I was standing there, and it quickly turned back into a frown. "You're still here?"

"The sword is old, and I know it's not going to be in there."

He sighed, walking across the room, throwing some things to the side, and picking up a large leather book. He walked back over to me, shoving the book towards me with no warning. I held on tight, trying not to drop it. I pushed it up my chest to get a better grip on it. "Every recorded weapon ever made is in that book. Read it." I moved to open the front of the book. "Not here!" he yelled before turning away from me.

I just rolled my eyes and listened to him. The second I stepped out of the room, the doors slammed shut and locked back up. For a short old man, he really can move fast.

I did my best to walk up the stairs and flip through the old pages of the book. There were so many weapons. For each one there was a sketch of the weapon, a description of it, and the level of skill needed to use it. It was remarkable, but something wasn't right. This was huge, but big enough to have a sword created so long ago…I didn't know.

"Looks like someone is studying." I jumped, quickly turning around to see Doan and Simone standing next to each other.

Doan looked as flashy as ever with his blonde hair cut short, but gold chains still prominent around his neck. A red and white cloak over his shoulders that matched his outfit. Even multiple rings on each hand, some I recognized and some I didn't.

Simone stood with his walking stick next to him, looking exactly the same except for the light gray against the darkness of his beard. He was dressed in all white, which contrasted nicely against his dark skin. Then I noticed something else that was different. The scars over his closed eyes were gone.

"She's noticing your eyes," Doan whispered, still loud enough for me to hear.

Simone chuckled. "Don't worry. I am still as blind as a cave fish. Just got rid of the scars."

"Well, you look just as handsome. I thought you two wouldn't be back from vacation for another week or so?"

"You haven't heard?" Doan asked. "Cordelia called upon us. Says she got some troubling news from the water droplets." Doan rolled his eyes.

"I don't know why you doubt her. Water is her specialty," Simone stated.

"And information is my job, and I don't have anything special to say."

Information! "We'll walk together!" I announced, getting both men to nod. I moved off to the side making sure to stand next to Doan. "Doan, you would consider yourself good at your job, correct?"

Simone scoffed.

Doan shot him a quick glare before looking over at me. "I consider myself the best in the business. What do you need?"

"I've been looking at all of the history books."

"I could tell someone has been studying." Simone said, "Your steps are more determined than before. Always happens when someone is learning more."

A smile spread across my face. Determined, yes.

"What are you looking for?" Doan asked.

"I'm looking for a weapon created a long time ago. Something that I don't think is in this book."

Doan paused for a moment, looking ahead. I noticed the way his eyes narrowed, that he had to be thinking. I noticed a servant walking past us, and I quickly stopped her. "Please bring this book to my room." I carefully handled the book so that she didn't drop it.

Then I continued walking with Doan and Simone, doing my best to ignore the aching screams in my arms. The inside of my elbows had turned red from how tightly I'd had to hold the book to keep from dropping it.

Whatever Doan was thinking, he hadn't said anything by the time we made it to the war room. "Maisey, I'm glad you made it," Cordelia said, getting my attention. The first thing I noticed when I looked at her was her blue hair braided over her shoulder, and then the bags under her eyes. She looked as if she hadn't slept in days. I knew what that was like.

"What's going on?" I asked as we walked into the room. Large marble columns outlined the inside of the room. In the center, under a large chandelier, was a round table where Grace and Jedediah were already waiting.

"I'm afraid that we are in big trouble." Cordelia walked us towards the table.

"I have heard nothing of the sort," Jedediah stated.

"Because I'm sure armies always let you know before they attack," Doan stated, rolling his eyes.

"Have you heard anything?" Grace asked Doan.

"Nothing, but peace."

I walked over to the large table, looking down at the map of Neville and surrounding kingdoms embedded in the table. It was all so beautifully detailed.

"Besides what happened at the church," Doan added.

My head quickly snapped toward Doan. "What happened?" I asked.

"Some tub thumper priest got attacked. He played like he didn't, but he's got one hell of a gash on his head."

I slightly nodded, looking back at the map. He better not say anything.

"I have listened to the water, I have listened to the forest, and our enemy doesn't come from a known kingdom," Cordelia contended in a harsh tone. "It is a toxin that wants to sink their teeth into the core of our kingdom and rip us apart from the inside out." When she spoke, her hands were shaking, I could hear the fear in her voice.

…Core of our kingdom…

The sword crafted in the core of the kingdom…

The castle! The sword was made in the castle from the souls of the innocent! That meant…possibly…I didn't know what that meant. I needed to look at that book again.

Then I heard a laugh, making me look up. It was a deep belly laugh coming from Jedediah. "You think there is a snake in the garden?" Jedediah asked.

"She is right," Simone said, getting everyone to look at him. "There is a change in the air." Simone tilted his chin up, taking a deep breath in and a pit in my stomach dropped to the floor. "A metallic smell. A calm before the storm." Simone opened his eyes, showing the deep blue color. "Chaos."

A terrifying silence drove into the room, sinking its teeth into me. Simone closed his eyes again, and suddenly I felt like all eyes were on me. Like they all knew what I was planning. Like they knew who the problem was. I carefully looked around the room, and no one was looking at me at all, but the worry on their faces was intense. "Doan," Grace cleared her throat, looking over at him. "Your job is information. I need you to find everything you can. We can't prepare if we don't know where this threat is coming from."

"Yes, your Grace." Doan slightly nodded, and then everyone seemed to go their separate ways. Everyone except for Cordelia.

She was just standing there, staring down at the map. I

walked over, standing closer to her. "Is there something you need to tell me?" I asked and her entire body started to tense, her eyes locking on the location of the castle. "Something you didn't tell everyone else because maybe…they wouldn't take it so well."

Cordelia opened her mouth, but no words seemed to leave her lips. "They don't believe in it." Cordelia whispered. "They don't believe in the world beyond ours."

"You mean the world beyond the veil?"

Cordelia looked up at me with glassy blue eyes. "It is dangerous. The monsters are forced to live through their biggest mistakes until it drives them mad."

"They aren't going to get out."

"You don't know that. There have always been gaps, especially on the castle ground, and they are getting bigger. Someone is poking the thin nets, and it's not from their side." A big tear slid down her cheek.

"Why the castle?"

Cordelia took a deep breath in, using her hand to wipe her cheeks. "It's where the veil was created. The castle was built around it."

"Everything is going to be fine. Maybe we can find a way to strengthen the hold of the veil, so everyone can feel protected."

Cordelia took a deep breath, slightly nodding her head. She opened her mouth to say something, but quickly closed it before walking out of the room. I looked back down at the map, staring at the castle itself. The monsters won't make it through the veil. I'm not that reckless. I will get Kit out and close it back up.

* * *

ALL DAY, the overwhelming feeling of disaster was the only thing in the castle. It was like a thick dark cloud over every single person. From those who knew what they were fearing and those who didn't. I couldn't risk letting anyone see me roaming the castle. So, I waited until night before I was able to go down the back stairs, holding a candle in my hand. There were candles on the wall for light, but no one was lighting them. No one was supposed to go down there. That became clear by all the webs and dust gathered around the walls and the mouse that ran past me on the stairs.

The only thing I could hear was the sound of the wind moving through the dark tunnel. The silence was deafening. At the end of the stairs was a brick wall. It was crumbling from time, but that wasn't all. I leaned forward, pressing my ear against the wall. Different and distant screams came from behind it. I put my hand against the wall, feeling a tingle travel through my fingers. Just as I was about to focus all my energy on the crumbling stone there was a deep cracking sound. I quickly moved away from the door, watching a crack move up from the ground. The crack continued to move, outlining the wall in the shape of a door. Once it made it to the ground on the other side, the makeshift door pushed itself open. The ground was nothing but sand and light stone. The air was cold, sending chills up my arm. The air went cold to the point I could see my own breath. I ran my hands over my arms, trying my best to create friction for warmth. In the center of the basement room was a large flattened stone. The only light came from the candle I was holding in my hands.

I moved around the flat stone and the air started to change. A warmth traveled up from the stone towards the ceiling above it. I slowly lifted my hand, hovering over the heat from a distance as it was rapidly getting hotter. The screams that seemed to drown in the chilling silence started to get louder. Not only were they getting louder, but they were saying something. I tried to hold onto what they were screaming but I couldn't. No matter how hard I tried to focus. It was just making my head hurt. I needed to find the sword. I followed the screams, bringing me to the wall in front of me. I ran my fingers against the stone, finding the crumbling pieces and picking at them more and more until the stone turned to give way.

Pain came from my fingers as I pushed into the stone. My nails broke from the pressure, but I didn't stop. I kept pushing up as the stone cleared away, and the sword was showing in its place. The handle was beautifully crafted with colors of red and black. The blade of the sword was black and vibrating from the voices coming from it. I lightly touched the cold metal of the blade, and the voices came clear...run! They were screaming at me to run. Fear rose inside of me, and I carefully backed away from the sword. I found it. I just needed to find it. I tried not to be scared, but that didn't explain why I was running my way back up the stairs. I ran so fast that my candle was no longer lit as I made it back to the main floors. I tossed the candle holder on a table in the hall, shaking the fear out of my hands. There was light in the halls and no screaming.

I went back into my bedroom to find it wasn't as empty as when I left it. Alice sat in my bed, dressed in a long black nightgown. Her back was against my headboard and legs stretched out in front of her. Sitting next to her legs was a light wooden tray holding two glasses and a kettle. "What are you doing in here?" I asked, walked over to her.

Alice slightly shrugged her shoulders. "I figured you would be up, and I brought some tea. With everything going on, I figured it would help with the stress."

I smiled at her, taking off my shoes and walking over to sit on the bed with her. Alice leaned forward, pouring me a glass of tea. "When was the last time you slept?" Alice asked, and I let out a deep breath, taking a drink of the warm liquid. I could feel its heat travel through my entire cold body all the way down.

"Sleep is for people who don't have anything to do," I stated, enjoying the cup with a quickness. A calm feeling traveled through me.

"I saw you in the garden one night." Alice said, making me look over at her. I don't remember being in the garden. A tingling feeling danced over my skin, and I finished the last of my tea before setting it on the tray. "I called your name. You didn't reply. You were just sitting there. Staring, mumbling. You weren't asleep, but you weren't here. I asked Tasar about it and he said it's from lack of sleep. You aren't giving yourself a break, so your magic is doing it for you. You don't think you're sleeping because in your head, you're not. The problem is the longer you go the harder it's going to be to tell what's real against what's not."

"It's not as…serious as he makes…sound." My words were slowing down like they couldn't form quickly enough. I rested my head against the headboard as my eyelids got heavy. I tried to hold them open, but the more I tried, the heavier they got.

"I'm sorry, but you can't go on like this." I heard Alice's voice, but I couldn't see her. I thought my eyes were open. I tried to look for her. Then a softness and warmth laid over me in utter comfort.

CHAPTER 13

Screams erupted from the empty castle halls as I ran through the darkness. I tried to follow the screams, to find someone—anyone to tell me what was happening. Every corner I turned trying to get closer to them seemed to only take me further away. All I knew was the fear deep in my gut that something terrible was happening.

The ground under me started to shake, getting more and more violent as I moved down the hall. I stumbled around the corner, falling into a pair of strong arms. It felt familiar. It felt safe. I knew that feeling. I let myself nuzzle into him. I stayed there, letting everything else disappear. There was no more screaming, there was no more shaking. A feeling of safety surrounding me.

Then a cold breeze sent chills down my arms. Suddenly, the warmth I felt was gone and replaced with a chill. I pulled back, looking up at him to feel my heart drop to the floor, shattering at my feet. His skin was a deadly pale, his brown eyes seemed to dull to a milky gray. Tears flooded my eyes, feeling his cold hand on my cheek. "I-I-I..." He took a deep breath in, fighting for his words. "I-I love you." I heard one final breath leave his lips. A loud shriek shot through the air, and I quickly covered my eyes, falling to my knees. A warm liquid fell against my fingers, unable to stop the high-pitched noise. Tears poured down my cheeks.

I shot up in a gasp, finding myself tucked into my bed, my body dripping with sweat. My red hair was sticking to my forehead, and the feeling of fear crawled its way up my body. The air around me thinned out, like it was being sucked away from me and a pain in my chest came from the pounding of my heart. I looked around at the quiet room and nothing seemed to be out of place but me. Then my brain snapped back to the warm tea I had drunk before. Alice's voice floated back to my memory. "I'm sorry, but you can't go on like this." My fingers wrapped around the blanket over me, the color leaving my knuckles.

I did my best to clean myself up before storming out of my bedroom. I had one person in my mind, but there was a part of me that didn't want to find her. I stormed through the castle, people moved themselves out of my way. Eventually, I found myself outside to see Alice near the castle pond feeding the ducks, pieces of bread in her hands. I knew I was angry before but seeing her sent a fury through me. Not like anything I felt before. Like the kind that made the power inside of me crave destruction. This anger came from the depths of my soul. "Alice!" I shouted, getting her to quickly turn around with wide blue eyes. "You drugged me!"

"I didn't drug you! I helped you get some sleep! You needed it!"

"You don't have the right to tell me what I need!"

Alice looked around, making sure we were alone as she stepped closer to me. "We have created a plan that is putting everything at risk. We need you at your best, and you're not."

"You think this is my best?" I asked through my teeth.

Alice took a deep breath, "I'm sorry—" Her words were

cut short by my hand striking her cheek. The tingling in my hand left me shocked. Alice looked up at me with tears pricking the corners of her eyes, redness quickly forming on her cheek. She had no right to tell you what you needed. For several seconds we just stared at each other before I turned away from her. I walked back into the castle, doing my best to ignore the doubt and anger that screamed at me.

I didn't need her. I didn't need anyone. I was the one who needed to do the spell, and that was exactly what I was going to do!

I stormed my way up the back staircase to my studio. I locked the door, pulled the book out, and set it on the table. I carefully flipped through the pages of the book, looking for the spell. I didn't need her! I didn't need anyone! I ignored the voices getting louder with every page I turned. I forced myself to focus through the screams all the way to the right page. There were too many voices for me to make out. I covered my ears, but it wasn't working. My dream flashed through my mind and my knees gave out, letting me drop to the ground. The darkness suffocated in its grasp.

My eyes shot open only to see a small piece of light breaking through the darkness. I was careful not to move because I didn't know what could be hiding in the darkness. That's when I heard it. The soft, beautiful voice of someone singing. I listened to the voice, unable to find the source. Then some more lights scattered around the darkness until the source found me. A woman appeared through the light, standing in front of me in a long, white dress. Her skin was a beautiful sun-kissed color. Her eyes, one blue and one green. Long black hair cascaded over her shoulders in waves all the way down to just above the floor. She ended her song, looking down at me with a soft smile. "Maisey." The way she spoke my name sent chills down my body.

"Who are you?" I asked, my voice shaking from the weight of her presence.

"I have many names, but I'm the one who created the veil."

Lady Ophelia—her journal was supposed to be giving me everything I needed to get Kit back.

She smiled at me. "That was my blessed name. The name given to me by the Gods."

"How are you here? Why are you here? Where am I?" The questions came out of me with no control. It was as if I was speaking them as soon as my brain thought of them.

"We are in your head. You kept ignoring my warnings, so I thought I would take a more upfront approach. I connected my spirit to this book to keep the world safe. It's not a peaceful afterlife, but we do what we must."

"Are you going to hurt me?"

She chuckled, holding out her hand. "If I didn't want you to find the book, you wouldn't have found it." I took her warm hand, letting her help me up. "The veil was a strong spell, but even the strongest of spells need a patch up every once a century."

"You want me to make it stronger?"

"I can't tell you how to do it, but I can warn you. The veil is filled with people that can't be let back onto your world. Some good people are forced into the veil, and I couldn't stop that. My heart weeps for them, but the good of the veil outweighs the bad."

"I'm not trying to get rid of the veil."

She nodded. "I know what you are planning to do, and I am warning you. People on the other side of the veil can't be trusted. They are corrupted. They are shattered in a way that can't be fixed."

My brain jumped to my own sickness. The same feeling the King said he felt. He understood that change. "I was dying before," I said. "It was my soul being sucked into the veil. Are you saying…"

"Yes, you are too, so imagine if that happened to a person without a heart to begin with. Imagine what they will do to the world. To the people you are supposed to look after."

"I-I don't want to hurt anyone."

She stayed silent, watching me. If she was going to say anything more, she kept it to herself. She just softly smiled at me, her head tilting up slightly. "And I hope you remember that on your journey."

I GASPED, shooting up on the cold wooden floor of my studio. I looked around to see the moon shining through the singular window. I pushed myself back against the wall to catch my breath. I would shut the veil and reinforce it. There had to be a way to make this easier. I didn't care about Odes and his plans. His plan was to get himself out of the veil. I can't do that. I looked up at the space in front of me. The secret hiding behind the walls. She knows more. She has to.

I stood up from the floor, walking across the room. Anna got monsters through the veil without a red moon. The secret door slammed open the second it appeared. My magic threw Anna up against the wall. The magic hovered over her throat as her feet struggled to feel the floor. "How did you crack the veil?" I asked, stepping closer to her. "Things were slipping through. There's got to be an easier way to do this. A faster way. A better way. You don't strike me as someone who would blindly follow someone without a plan!"

"Magic not being what you thought?" I could hear the enjoyment in her strained voice, and I dropped her back down to her feet. Anna bent forward, holding her throat as she coughed. "You're right. I know of other ways, but there are no easier ways!" Anna caught her breath, looking up at me as she rested her head back against the wall. "Especially not for you."

"What does that mean?"

Anna chuckled. "You were born with unspeakable power. A power that would drive the strongest people…" Anna paused, her stare turning cold. "Well, I think you know that one. You're getting too comfortable with the violence of your magic. It feels good, doesn't it? Knowing no one can tell you no. No one can tell you what to do." She took in a deep breath, pushing herself up off the wall. "I had to steal my magic. You can't do that. You can't forge something new when what you have doesn't match up." She looked towards the fireplace, watching the flames crackle against the wood. A small smirk tugged at the corner of her lips as a spark lit in her dark eyes. "Pulling things out was like trying to thread a needle without being able to see. Kind of why I had to drain the kingdom's magic. If our world was weak enough, I could get the thread through." Anna's eyes flickered back up at me, her face hardening against any more enjoyment. "You're out of your depths, child. What he's trying to get you to do will destroy you and everyone around you." I looked back up at Anna as she motioned toward herself. "I think I would know. So, you need to decide right now how much that hunter means to you."

I glared at her, refusing to let her see how much her words shook me to my core. I stepped out of the room, letting the door shut and disappear into the magic behind me.

You're getting too comfortable with the violence of your magic. It feels good, doesn't it? Knowing no one can tell you no. No one can tell you what to do.

Everything I'd done. All the chaos around me. All I had been trying to do was right what I did wrong, and I had just been making everything worse. I even hurt someone who was only trying to help me.

MORNING CAME and there was one thing left for me to do. My anger was drained, and I was left with my fear and doubt. The feelings I deserved. The door opened and Tasar's face only slightly softened. I put my hands up in surrender. "I mean no harm," I said, and Tasar sighed, stepping to the side to let me into the room. Alice sat on one of the tables, a cloth in her hand and a red mark still on her cheek from the gold and red ring I was wearing. It was getting better, but it shouldn't have happened in the first place. My eyes struggled to focus on her. "I'm sorry about how I reacted. You were trying to help me, and I hurt you."

"You don't hit that hard."

"Doesn't make me any less sorry," I let out a deep breath, looking down at my hands. "Anna told me I am going to destroy myself and everyone I care about, and I think she's right."

"No, she's not."

I shook my head, struggling to get my words out. "I've been having nightmares. Bad ones. They are…so real and I'm trapped, and even when I wake up, I'm still living that over and over again, and I know the second I close my eyes I'm going to be back there. I can't—I just can't!" My words came out louder than I intended, and I quickly closed my eyes tightly, pressing my fingers against the corners of my eyes trying to stop the tears before they could escape.

"We are going to fix it, but we can't if you keep punishing yourself," Alice said.

"As far as the nightmares," Tasar said, standing near the door. "I'll give you something. It will block them. You won't have dreams, but it might be better than what you are having."

I nodded slightly. "Thank you."

Alice gave me a soft smile. "Now, we can go catch ourselves a unicorn."

THE SEALS COME **from others with matching power of the first witch.** — That's me.

A single vial of the first marked. — I will be given that last by Odes.

The heart of the uncorrupted in a world filled with torment. — We still needed it.

The sword crafted in the core from the souls of the innocent. — I know where the sword is waiting for me.

Under the red moon in the site of creation is the seal of those lost. — That is coming.

WE WERE SO CLOSE. We were so close to having it all.

CHAPTER 14

lice went back to the Inn to send the girls on a mission. It took them a couple days, but now we had the information that we needed.

His name was Illios, he worked in a little shop, and spent his nights wasted and in the Inn. He had been detained six times for thievery and fights. He was out now and just lost his job because the last arrest he had was from fighting inside the shop with one of the customers.

When Alice and I traveled with cloaks over our heads under the darkness of the night sky, we made a decision not to tell Tasar until it was over. "All he's going to do is complain and tell us what we are doing wrong," Alice stated, rolling her eyes. I followed her all the way to the little shack house Illios was living in. She snuck her way towards the window, pulling the shutters open, showing there was no actual glass, and jumped in with no hesitation.

"Why are we breaking into his…home?" I asked, standing on the other side of the window, while Alice was standing in the center of his small bedroom.

"The heart of the uncorrupted in a world filled with torment." She recited one of the ingredients from the book.

"Yeah, that still doesn't answer my question. Shouldn't we wait for him to get home?"

Alice stared at me, confused. "Why would we wait for him to be here? So he can hear us stealing from him?"

"Why do I feel like we aren't talking about the same thing?"

"Get in here before someone sees you!"

I sighed, climbing up the window, and Alice helped me through to the other side. She made it look so much easier. I got into the room, now crowded with both of us in there. Alice slid around me, closing the shutters of the window. "How is breaking into his house going to get us his heart?" I asked, and Alice stared at me with a blank look on her face.

"Maisey, unicorns don't have hearts like us. A unicorn's heart is what they care about most. The source of their power." Alice pointed at her own forehead.

"Their horn?" I asked and Alice nodded.

"Yes," Alice's eyes went wide. "Did you really think we were going to rip out someone's heart?"

"I thought it was weird you guys were so cool with the idea, but I wasn't really trying to talk about it!"

"Goddess Almighty, Maisey!"

"No one explained it! I also don't understand why the horn isn't on his body!"

Alice shrugged slightly, looking around the room. "There are many different guesses as to why, but I wasn't there to know for sure. The one that makes the most sense is that they were being hunted, and the magic coming off their horns is too easily tracked when they were connected to the body, so they took them off. Now, are you going to help me search or are you going to make me do this all myself?"

I pressed my lips together, kicking through the dirty piles

of clothes, peeking inside boxes scattered around the room, and moving things out of the way. "How do you even know that it's going to be here?"

"I asked one of the girls to express that she needed to hide something important to her, and he said to keep it somewhere you can visit without drawing suspicion. One place you can visit every day that no one is going to think twice about...a bedroom. You have to sleep, you know that better than anyone."

I remember hiding things from the other kids in the foster homes I was in. Some were just curious, but others would use the thing you valued most in the world to mess with you. Your bedroom was as close to private as you could get, but you had to get creative if you were going to hide something from room/bed checks. I hid my things under my bed. Not on the ground where it could be found, but...

I picked up the mattress off the floor, running my hands over the back until I found a small opening. I pushed my hand into the opening until I felt something hard in the cushion of the bed. I took hold of the hard cylinder shape, pulling it out of the mattress. When I got a look at what I had found, I saw that it was a horn, shining through the multiple colors of the rainbows that moved from the bottom to the tip in gentle waves. It still sparkled even though we were standing in the darkness. Then we heard loud cursing coming from outside the shack. I quickly fixed the bed. "We got to go!" I urgently whispered, re-opening the shutters of the window, and climbing out. I hid the horn in my cloak, keeping the natural light coming off it from being spotted in the darkness. Alice took my arm, pulling me back into the bushes we hid in before. Once we were in the bushes, we were able to escape into the woods and to the horses we tied up to wait for us.

There was only one thing left. A single vial of the first

marked. One thing left and I would be able to fix the biggest mistake I had ever let happen.

I brought the horn back up to my studio, hiding it in a small box I placed inside the floor. I moved the basket, putting it on top of the hole. Then like clockwork, a breeze moved through the room. Odes was standing in the center of the room when I stood up from the floor. "We are one step closer," I said, walking over to sit on the table in front of me.

"What else do you need?"

"Just the vial of the first marked."

He nodded, clasping his hands behind his back as he watched me. "You won't be able to get another one. You'll get it when we are closer to the red moon."

I could feel myself starting to get annoyed. I had already hit enough of my own delays, I didn't want to have to deal with his too. "Why don't you want me to get it sooner?" I asked, crossing my arms over my chest.

"It's not about what I want. It's about what will work."

"I have found everything I needed, and you don't think I can take care of a vial of blood."

"It's not blood," he snapped quickly, clenching his jaw after he said it.

"What is it?"

He looked away from me, "Something stronger than blood, and contrary to what you keep suggesting, I am only trying to give us both the best chance to get what we want."

I stood up from the table, stepping closer to him. "What do you want?"

He didn't look at me. "I want to go home."

"How did you get to the other side of the veil?" I wanted to read his face, but he wouldn't meet my gaze. I needed to know where his lies were. I had to know what I needed to be prepared for. Lady Ophelia's voice ran through my head. "People on the other side of the veil can't be trusted. They are corrupt. They are shattered in a way that can't be fixed."

"I was betrayed by someone I loved. Someone I thought loved me."

"Who?"

He finally looked at me, but his gaze wasn't telling anything. He was reading me. Reading me the same way I was reading him. "Why the sudden interest in my history?"

"Why are you avoiding it?" I asked, holding my gaze against his. His was strong. The gold in his eyes shot daggers into me. "All this time you have known more about me than I have about you. I think it's time we change that if you want to come back into my kingdom." Odes chuckled, turning away from me and walking across the room to the single window. "What's so funny?"

"I doubt you would have said my kingdom when you were first thrown into this world."

"That observation doesn't change a thing."

Odes let out a deep breath, staring outside the window. "When we are brought into the world, we are dependent on the people that create us. I didn't have parents who cared. I had to find that connection from somewhere else. Somewhere with more…power, but with that power came rules. It didn't matter what was right or wrong, if you broke their rules, you were to be punished."

"What rule did you break?"

He looked back at me. He may not have told the truth the entire time, but he was this time. "An unjust one."

"Do you have anyone waiting for you to come back?"

"Are you asking if I plan on causing problems upon my return?"

I sighed, deciding not to agree with him completely. "I'm asking if you have a plan. I doubt it will be easy adjusting once you're back."

He slightly nodded, choosing to accept my answer. "It is not your concern. Once I am out, you will never see me again." That's what I wanted. When this was all over, I wanted nothing to remind me of what I had to do to get there. I didn't want to remember who I hurt or who I manipulated to get what I wanted.

* * *

I WANTED to forget what Odes had told me before. I wanted to keep moving forward, but that wasn't going to happen any time soon. I was stuck replaying our conversation, replaying the look in his eyes, replaying the chills his very presence sent through my body. Something was wrong. I needed to know more, and there was only one person that would know him better than I did. I walked into the room shutting the door behind me. Anna, who was sitting in her chair with a book in her lap, let out a deep breath at my arrival. "I need to ask you something and I want the truth. No work around, no riddles, no hold backs. I want the complete truth."

Anna sighed, shutting the book in her lap. "Please, I would love to chat."

"Do you understand me?" I asked.

"As long as I get the same."

I rolled my eyes, deciding to move on. I just needed to know what I needed to know. Even if that meant I needed to be honest with the woman that I hated. "What did Odes say he was going to do when he got out of the veil?"

"You think he told me his plans?"

"I think you always know more than you let on. I think you have your suspicions, and I think he told you what you could expect."

Anna paused for a moment, staring at me. "I don't know

why I thought you were so stupid." Anna slightly scoffed, not waiting for me to reply. "I think it was the love thing."

"Answer my question."

"He only told me what he thought I needed to know, but he did tell me once he was out of the veil, I would be his queen. I would get everything I wanted and everything that was taken from me." I felt all the color leave my face as I thought about what he said to me. He promised I would never see him again. Anna was watching me and reading me like the book sitting in her lap. "He promised you the opposite. Makes sense. It is the first rule of manipulation. Make sure the person gets what they want most. You don't want him, I did. I feel sorry for you."

"You're trapped in a room with no way out, and you feel sorry for me?"

"Yes. You couldn't learn everything the normal way, and now you are drowning in your own mistakes. I get it. Your mother won't, but I do."

I shook my head, walking towards the door. I was only able to touch the doorknob when her voice got my attention again.

"If you are starting to wonder if you made a deal with the devil, you did. If you think you can get out of it, you can't."

I looked back at Anna and the cocky smile plastered on her face. She thought she was beating me again. That I didn't list the possibilities laid out in front of me. "I knew the deal I was making," I stated, walking out of the room and shutting the door behind me. I knew where these choices were leading me. He's a liar, but so am I.

CHAPTER 15

I was in the castle kitchen putting different herbs and flowers into a stone bowl. I was following an old recipe in one of the many books I took from the library. It took me hours to figure out what I needed, but once I did, there was a certain pride in it. The castle was silent from everyone else's ability to sleep. The only thing to listen to was the sound of my own movement around the kitchen.

It's amazing what they have been able to figure out. The different drinks and foods and medicines they have created with just a splash of magic to help their people...but they never crossed the line. They never worked to play God in their hopes of helping people. They weren't bringing back the dead. They weren't messing with fate.

Not like me.

I tried hard not to think about my life before I even ended up in Neville. When I did think about it, my stomach tensed up in a giant knot and a bitter taste filled my mouth. I didn't do much before all of this, but I didn't feel this way either. You can't feel loss if you have nothing to lose.

I was dying...it was hard to think about that now, but

it's the truth. The life was being sucked out of me. It was hard to imagine that the only crime I committed to deserve all that was being born. It amazed me that a baby could cause so much hate, but...it wasn't really a hate. It was pain. A pain that ate away at every moral or belief you had before. A pain that took and took until you were willing to do anything and everything to make it go away.

That's where I am.

I didn't want to feel this anymore. I couldn't feel this way anymore. The time was coming faster and faster and when it did...I would be done. I would be putting all of this behind me and never looking back. I didn't care about power. I didn't care about the chaos. I didn't care about Anna, or what the hell would happen to her. Once I fixed what I had done, there would be nothing left for me to do. I didn't even care about the crown.

I knew Grace wanted me to, and there was a part of me that didn't want to disappoint her. She's been good to me. We fought a lot in the beginning, but she lost someone she cared about, and I lost someone I cared about. That type of loss changes people. I became her focus, and she did everything she thought I would need, but it didn't change the fact I have been alone all my life.

I finished the recipe, pouring the liquid into the teapot. I set the teapot onto the stove and with a quick light of the pilot there was only the job of waiting a little longer. Only more time to be stuck in my own head.

Which is never fun.

"I'm pretty sure a princess doesn't need to make tea." I jumped at the sound of Grace's voice.

I slightly chuckled at my own fear. "Says the Queen."

Grace let out a deep breath, "Cordelia's fear of another war is making it hard to sleep."

I nodded. "I'm sure she's just...unsettled. We all have been."

"Speaking of which, there is something I want to discuss with you, and I would like you to listen to me this time." Grace stepped forward, standing in front of me with just the counter to separate us. "We haven't had this conversation since the first time and there is something I want to tell you..." Grace took in a deep breath before continuing. "It's about you getting married."

I quickly shook my head, pulling out a carrying tray and setting a teacup onto it. "I don't want to talk about this again," I quickly stated.

"I know, and I get it."

I let out a deep breath, forcing myself to look up at her. "Do you?"

"You lost someone that you love."

My body quickly tensed. I had gotten so used to focusing on my goal instead of the reason this entire situation was happening in the first place.

"But you can't fight off happiness forever. I'm just asking that you go into your coronation with an open heart. A chance to meet someone that can make you happy. Maybe it's just a friendship, but you never know what can happen."

"You say that like I'm not happy."

"You're as happy as I am."

I let out a deep breath, opening my mouth but was instantly cut off by the sound of the teapot screaming. I walked over, setting the tea on a tray before picking it up. "I will consider it," I lied, walking out of the kitchen. If she wanted to stop me, she didn't. I made my way through the empty castle, but I wasn't going to my bedroom. I was going to see Anna. Something told me she was going to enjoy this tea.

I made it just for her.

I walked into Anna's room to see her pacing in front of the fire. She straightened her back, gripping the shelf of the fireplace with one hand while the other pushed her hair back and out of her face. I heard her taking in a deep breath, cracking her neck side to side before turning to look at me. She looked annoyed, judging by the rage in her eyes, but the smirk on her face told me she was satisfied to see me. It made me wonder how alone she felt when I shut this door behind me.

"You brought me tea?" Anna asked as I adjusted the tray in my arm, to place my hand flat on the door as I pushed it shut. A tingling burn came from my hand, an invisible symbol carving into the wood. "Why?" Anna asked, and I moved my hand, walking over to set the tray on the table next to her chair.

"We need to talk."

Anna scoffed, "And this is what? A peace offering? Trying to make us a part of a family again."

I scoffed. "A peace offering suggests I care about peace between us, and I couldn't care less about that. We never were a family, and we never will be." I walked away from the tray and made my way around the room. Anna was too busy focusing on whatever was going on in her head to worry about what I was doing. Instead of watching me, she looked back at the fire, staring at the dancing flame. I walked to the wall across from the door, placing my hands behind the dark curtains. On this end, there was no window, only the wood of the walls, but maybe on her end there was. The end I didn't see when I closed this door. Heat came from my hand burning another invisible symbol into the wood.

"That's not how you are supposed to treat your family." Sarcasm filled her voice as she plopped herself into her chair, picking up my tea pot.

I moved around the room casually. Anna's back was to me

as I stood behind her chair in front of the small, hanging bookcase. Anna chuckled slightly, I'm sure from a joke in her own head. I wondered if she could feel what I was doing. I moved my hand between the books and placed my hand in the same way I had before.

Anna looked around the tray as I moved around towards the fireplace in the front of the room. "What no sugar?" Anna asked, raising a brow towards me.

"You want sugar?" I asked, raising my brow back at her as I casually placed my flat hand on the grooves carved into the fireplace just under the shelf. Every carving aligned with one another. They connected like chains to hold a veil of privacy.

Anna chuckled, looking down at the cup of tea before drinking it. "Look who knows me better than I thought." She threw one leg over the other under her long, black dress. Once the carvings were placed, I finally let myself look at her. She seemed as if she had changed so fast since the last time I saw her. It didn't feel possible, but I didn't know what happened once I shut this door behind me. I didn't even think about it. She was so thin, so pale, her long black hair was lying in strands in front of her face.

She looked like she was dying.

"What happens to this room when I leave?" I finally asked, getting her to look back up at me.

"What do you mean?"

"The curtains. Clearly there has to be a window on the other side for you. I want to know what else is. Like, what replaces the door I use to talk to you when I leave."

"Not much. A cell. Better than the one before. I got a bed. Working on getting a bathroom that isn't in the same room. Talking to you does get me more to bargain for."

I couldn't stop the soft laugh that escaped.

"Something funny?"

"He's bribing you to know what is said between us." I

slightly shrugged. "Odes kind of seems like the man who has ears everywhere. Why would he need to bribe you?"

"Who said that was what he was bribing me for?" Anna held a smirk as she took another sip of her tea. "This is rather good. What kind of poison did you use?"

"I didn't poison you." Flashes of Anna and her heart, each falling to the stone ground in front of me. "You don't have a heart, literally. Can I even kill you?"

Anna paused for a moment, thinking over my question. "That's a good question. I honestly don't know. That's one thing I never needed to know."

Who said that was what he was bribing me for? Anna's voice played in my head.

"What is Odes bribing you for?" I asked.

"To keep my mouth shut."

"And you'd just tell me that."

"He didn't give me anything to not tell you that." Anna finished her tea before refilling her cup again. I'm not surprised about any of this. He controlled Anna more than I ever could, but the pit in my stomach told me to leave. Told me something was wrong. Deciding to listen to this voice, I turned on my heel, quickly walking towards the door. I was only able to touch it when my entire body froze at her voice. "Do you ever wonder why he's in the veil?" Anna asked, and I held my breath.

I could tell by her voice she was no longer talking about Odes. "I already know. He can't find peace. He can't move on."

"He wouldn't be the first person that can't find peace, and they don't end up stuck in that type of torture."

My mouth instantly went dry. A sour feeling moved through my entire body. It was as if my body knew what she was going to say before the words left her mouth.

"I mean, who benefited if he was in the veil?" Anna paused. "Very curious. Don't you think?"

My entire body started to shake. I quickly stepped out of the room, slamming the door behind me. I couldn't stop the shaking. I couldn't stop the anger moving like a hurricane under my skin. Who benefited if he was in the veil...Who benefited... I felt as if my entire body wanted to scream. I could barely hold onto my breath as I tried to push down the rage. It wanted to tear everything apart. To make everyone feel the pain that was suffocating me.

NO! The voice inside of me shouted. The voice didn't just shout at me but stopped everything around it. It stopped the hurricane, stopped the hot tears from falling down my cheeks, stopped the rage. That won't get me anything. That won't get me what I want. That won't give me the revenge that I desire. You want pain...I will show you pain.

I looked over at the small mirror hanging in the room, to the red eyes staring back at me. This voice in my head...it didn't feel like mine because it wasn't mine. It was the power inside of me. It was the chaos desiring to be free...And I was listening to it.

CHAPTER 16

The moon was high in the sky when Odes appeared in my bedroom. He told me to grab my cloak, and I followed him out of the castle. Every turn or covering that the moon couldn't reach made him vanish into the air. When that happened, all I could do was follow the sound of his voice, leading me away from the castle. Most of what he said was rambling. Rambling about this beautiful home he once knew. A home that was filled with laughter and love during the day and utter terror at night.

I stopped listening to him. Listening to him was exhausting. I didn't care about what he had to say. I didn't want to pretend to care about some story that he had. I only wanted to see him hurt. I wanted him to feel what I felt.

Eventually, after what felt like hours, we finally stopped in front of the dark run-down cabin buried into the tall forest trees. Trees have grown through it to the point it was lopsided. The wood was dark and rotten. If it was a home, it hadn't been in a very long time. "What is this place?" I asked.

"Go inside." Odes stood next to me, staring at the house like he could see something I couldn't, and whatever he was seeing…he didn't like. "In the back of the main room, under the only straight floorboard is a black metal box, it has symbols all over it, open it, and take out the vial."

I had only taken a few steps towards the door when I realized he was still standing there, staring at it. "You were paranoid about me getting this, and you aren't going to go with me?" I asked, but he didn't look at me.

"I can't go inside." His stare was cold, but the clenching of his jaw was…pain. I could have asked, but I didn't feel sorry enough to care.

"I'll see you when I come back," I stated, stepping closer to the house. "I better not fall through the floor!" I shouted back at him as I carefully stepped on the still-solid porch boards despite the instability of them all. I focused on every creak and movement as I made my way inside. I walked towards the back of the cabin when I felt a snap under my foot dropping me to the ground. Pain from the broken wood that scraped against my leg made me wince as I pulled it back up. I looked at the room around me. Old chairs were turned over, I even spotted what looked like an old mug on the floor against the wall, but everything was covered in dirt, cobwebs, and the forest had made its way inside. I groaned, looking at the back of the cabin and noticed that there was only one board that wasn't slanted, broken, or brittle. Only one that was still fresh. The wood had darkened from the exposure to the elements, but it wasn't rotten.

I pushed myself up, getting my leg out of the hole. Instead of standing only to end up with another foot in a hole, I crawled across the floor to the floorboard. I wedged my finger into the gap between this floorboard and the broken one next to it. I pulled and pulled and got nothing. "It's not coming up!" I shouted. I waited for an answer and got nothing. I sighed, dropping my hands into my lap. Magic! "Duh!" I rolled my eyes, surprised that I didn't realize it sooner. I watched the red mist leave my fingers, wrap itself around the gaps of the floorboard, and I pulled it out with a snap. Like I was told, I saw a black box sitting there with white markings all over it. I reached in to pick up the box. Instead of feeling the coldness of the metal, I felt an intense heat burning my hand forcing me to drop the box. I shook my hands, holding my breath until the pain went away. Once all the heat went away, I looked back at the box. Odes's instructions replayed in my head.

He didn't say touch it. He said open it. Using my magic again, I slowly lifted the lid to see a single vial of blood sitting on top of red silk cushioning inside. I could tell there was an indent where another vial had been. I used my magic to lift the vial, holding my breath until it was out of the box and high enough that I could take it in my hand.

I had it! I had the last piece of the puzzle! Then like a cough I couldn't shake, Anna's voice played through my head again.

Who benefited if he was behind the veil?

It took everything I had not to crush it in my hand. This could give him pain. He may not have been able to get it himself, but this mattered to him. He could cover it up and deny it, but this was his last chance.

I carefully made my way back outside to Odes, still standing where he was before. "Did you get it?" Odes pried his eyes from the house, finally looking at me.

"Yes," I answered, swallowing down the bitter taste in my mouth.

Who benefited if he was behind the veil?

I moved my hands behind my back. I could feel the vial shift in my hand. Once I settled it, I held it in my fingers, holding it out in front of him. He looked down at the vial. I dropped it into my palm, closing my fingers around it. He gave me a questioning look. "Did you know that killing Anna would put Kit into the veil?" I asked, watching his face as closely as I could.

"How would I know that?" Odes asked, taking a step towards me, and I held my fingers tighter.

I shook my head, feeling my eyes turn red. "I don't believe you. I think you always know more than you let on." I heard the snap of the glass in my palm, the blood dripping from between my fingers onto the dirt.

"NO!" Odes's scream was power and rage. Odes looked at me with the gold in his eyes flaring. His entire body was shaking. I could feel the weight of his power radiating off him. He stepped towards me, trying to intimidate me. He would have before. The girl that showed up here with no idea where she was and wanted nothing more than to make it back to Maine…she would have been terrified. "What did you do?" he asked through his teeth. I could see the fire behind his eyes. The rage…the pain…the wish for blood.

With a little satisfaction, I pulled out my other hand, opening it to show the real vial in my hand. He looked down at the vial before his eyes traveled back to mine. "You keep clenching your jaw so hard, your teeth are going to fall out," I stated, and he looked away from me, softly shaking his head. "I've been learning a few things. Parlor tricks really." I looked down at my other hand that once had blood on it to see nothing. I watched Odes run his hand over his face. "I wanted to prove a point."

Odes scoffed, snapping over to stare at me. "What was the point of risking something we both want!" Odes shouted, and I was the one who took a threatening step towards him.

"That fear you had, the pain you felt is just a FRACTION of what I've been feeling since you took Kit from me! We are not friends! We are not partners! The second this is over, I am coming after you, and you will be the one wishing we never met!"

He stared back at me, neither of us breaking the power struggle between us. "No one threatens me," he spoke through his teeth yet again.

"And yet, I just did."

BY THE TIME I got back to the castle, the sun was just starting to rise. With everything we needed for the spell, Alice, Tasar, and I headed down to the basement. They followed me down the old narrow staircase to the different brick wall at the end. I placed my hand on the sides, feeling it start to move like it did before. Prying itself open, letting us all inside. This time was different. First, the door opened easier now than it had before. I couldn't hear the screams like I had before. The silence was thick. "This isn't terrifying," I heard Alice say quietly. She was right. This was worse than before. The silence…it could scare the strongest of people.

We each stepped on to the sand floor under us. Tasar walked around the room, lighting the old torches to give us more light. The sword was still in the stone where I left it last time I was down here. Looking at it sent chills down my arms. I could still spot my blood on the stone from prying it out.

Once there was enough light, Tasar walked over to the sword, staring at it. He stepped closer before quickly jumping back.

"What's wrong?" Alice asked, quickly stepping behind me.

"I-I heard…" Tasar was breathing heavily as he tried to get the words out.

"Screaming," I stated, and his head snapped towards me.

"A sword that screams?" Alice asked from behind me.

"The sword crafted in the core from the souls of the inno-cent." I recited the book's own words.

"And the innocent souls are screaming?" Alice's voice was quiet with fear. "Are they saying something or just screaming in fear?"

"Come here, and you can listen for yourself," Tasar stated and I looked back at Alice who just quickly shook her head.

I walked over with a small box in my hand, setting it under the point of the sword. In the box was the vial of blood that I needed. Tasar handed me the wrapped-up unicorn horn in order to avoid stepping closer to the sword again. I could feel the voices coming from the sword, but they weren't as loud as before. It was as if they just wanted to make sure I knew they were there. They no longer warned me. They just didn't want to be forgotten. I looked up at the sword, holding my breath. It was beautiful and had a shine to it that made me want to take it with me. "The power coming off this sword beats like a heartbeat," I said, my voice coming out as a whisper.

"Is that a bad thing or a good thing?" Alice asked, her feet still planted where I left her.

"It's neither," Tasar answered. "It just is."

"Okay, now that we have everything, and the location, can we leave now?" Alice asked, and I looked at her, opening my mouth just as the sound of a loud slam hit my ears. Alice whipped around, running towards the now-closed brick door. "This is bad! This is bad! This is bad!"

"Panicking isn't helping!" Tasar stated and Alice snapped towards him.

"Don't you think that if I could control my panic I would!" Alice yelled at him.

"Everything is fine!" I yelled, getting them both to look at me. While Alice felt we were trapped, I saw this as a warning. They didn't want me to do the spell. No one wanted me to do the spell. Each was trying to warn me, but none would succeed. It was almost over. Soon I would have everything I wanted. Soon everything would be right again. I looked back at the sword, my eyes glowing red. "Enough!" I shouted in demand, and after a moment of heavy silence, I heard the sound of the door slowly opening again. The second I turned around, Alice was already running up the stairs. Tasar was not far behind her.

I walked out of the stone room, stepping on the narrow staircase and the door closed again. I made it upstairs where they were both waiting for me. "And you act like I'm the only one that was freaking out!" Alice yelled at him.

"I was fine! You're the one yelling!" Tasar stated, clearly defensive.

"You were freaking out," I stated as I walked past them.

"Ha!" Alice cheered, and I pressed my lips together to fight my own laughter. I felt lighter as I moved down the hall.

We're...so...close.

CHAPTER 17

'I never planned on writing this down. It was my wish to do what the Gods have wished and move forward. Let the truth of the veil hide where no creature could unleash it or what it holds. Yet, the Gods say I must. I must state with as much force as I hold in my heart that the veil must be closed before it opens in its entirety. To close the veil, I will draw my blood along the opening, creating a seal on both sides. Doing this will leave me trapped on the other side with no way out. Trapped with the one person that would like nothing more than to kill me. The other way will take too long. Creatures will get through, creatures that I am doing all of this to get rid of. The power it would take to melt the sword of innocent souls over the opening would be too risky and would take everything I had. I cannot fail. If I failed, no one would be able to save the people of this world.'

I READ through Lady Ophelia's own notes in the darkness of my studio deep into the night. She knew the dread herself.

She knew the truth behind her own words. She knew what her power could do. She had time to learn it in a way I never would. When it came to my magic, I was always the one running to try to catch up. I didn't grow up with this storm of chaos…well, I did, but I didn't know what it was. I just thought it was the curse I was destined to live through. Maybe it still is. I was taking down the border to a world of monsters, and I just declared war against someone much more powerful than myself. That was what I had done. That was the legacy I would leave behind.

We all had a legacy to leave behind.

Chills ran up and down my spine as I looked up from the pages. Odes stood in the center of the room with his arms crossed, glaring at me with his golden eyes filled with rage. "You are wasting time," he spoke through clenched teeth, and I rolled my eyes, resting my hands on the table.

"For someone who can't do anything, you are being very controlling."

"If you fail—"

"Save the empty threat. You and I both know you can't do anything to me if I fail."

He walked over to the table, standing across from me. He was used to holding all the power, and I was testing him. "Do you enjoy being a pain?" he asked with a slight smirk forming on his face. "It's said that there's a fine line between love and hate."

"Don't make me hurt you."

He chuckled, making my hand twitch with an urge to smack him. "You can't hurt me. You can do to me as much as I do to you." That struck my interest. He was here and not here at the same time, but he was stronger than I had been when I went into the veil. I had touched him. His touch had been light, more of a presence than a real touch, but I swore that I touched him. Maybe it was different coming here than it was going there. Maybe being here made him stronger than being there.

"What a shame," I stated. When I looked up, he was gone, and my body tensed. I felt a cold breeze behind me, and I quickly turned. "Then don't stand so close. I prefer my space."

He was still smirking at me. He was enjoying this. He didn't care about how upset I was. He thrived on it. "You shouldn't show your emotion on your face. It makes you vulnerable." He moved past me, looking down at the book on the table as he moved.

"I really don't like you," I mumbled, turning away from him.

"I'm starting to feel the same," he stated before disappearing back into the darkness.

I could feel a raging fire building inside of me all over again. It felt like it wanted nothing more than to get out. Like it was screaming and begging to make everything go away. Going away in a ball of fire seemed to be the only way it found suitable. The type of fire that was threatening to burn me from inside out.

I looked back down at the book in front of me. I need...I need...I needed to see Kit. That was what I needed. I walked back over to the table, aggressively opening it back up. I didn't need to listen. He's not in charge. He can't tell me anything more now that I don't already know. My rage found a way to fuel me as I continued through the pages until I found what I needed. It was a way for me to project myself through the veil like I had done before. This time Odes wasn't going to be here, getting in my head. Anything we said to each other was going to stay between us. I just wanted to see him. I just wanted to remind myself why I was doing all of this. Remind me why I was willing to risk it all.

* * *

I OPENED MY EYES, seeing the dull grass under my feet. The trees around me were dark and so, so tall, they looked like they were just about to touch the sky. It all seemed so unreal. Because it was. For me this was just a vision. It wasn't my reality. I couldn't be killed or hurt. I could see and talk. I was there and not there all at the same time. I looked at the trees around me. It was so quiet that it sent chills up my arms. There were no sounds of birds, no leaves moving from the wind, hell, there was no wind. Then I heard the sound of a loud growl sticking fear through my entire body. I instinctively jumped back just as a large white beast, double the size of the large man it was wrestling, appeared. I watched the man stab his dagger into the head before taking another to plunge into its heart. There was a sharp sound of a painful screech before the silence came back. I stood there soaking in the silence as I watched the man standing. His height, his pulled back dark hair, the broadness of his shoulders, and the memorable tattoos…

"Kit!" I called out just as he pulled the dagger out of the large beast lying on the ground next to him. He stared at the beast, but he was listening to me. "Kit!" I called out again and he turned slowly, holding the knife tightly in his hand as he turned to look at me. This gave me a proper look at him. His dark-brown eyes were wide with wildness. He was covered in dirt and old blood. His clothes were ripped, and his hair was pulled back for the most part, but a lot of it had fallen out of place. My heart sank to see him this way. I took a step forward and his body tensed, making me halt. "Kit, it's me."

"I will not be fooled by this again!" he shouted at me, and I saw the way he twisted the knife in his hand. "You're not here."

I put my hand up as a way of surrendering as I cautiously

walked towards him. "I am and I'm not. I could only project myself here, but I had to talk to you. It's not very easy or I would have done it sooner." He let me get close enough to stand in front of him, but he was watching me very carefully.

I could see the hurt in his eyes. "The things you want most. The people you wish to see again are always what it shows you the most. You can't sleep without being reminded of everything you lost. They show it and show it until it drives you as crazy as all the things that try to kill you."

I felt a warm tear slide down my cheek. I wanted to touch him. To let him know it was going to be okay, but I couldn't. I couldn't touch him this way. I couldn't look after him this way. "I am so sorry you are going through this."

"There is nothing to be sorry for. When I followed you to that mountain, I knew I was either going to walk away with you or I was going to die trying."

I quickly shook my head. "You shouldn't have to live like this—" My voice caught in my throat like the wind had been knocked out of me. My whole body started to shake, and my heart started pounding. "I have to go now, but we will see each other again. I will fix everything I did wrong!"

"Maisey—"

I WAS THROWN BACK into my studio, slamming onto the hardwood floors. I gasped for air, feeling as if there was none around me. I put my hand over my heart, focusing on my breathing the best I could. The air around me was so cold. My breath slowly went back to the way it was supposed to be. I turned onto my side, wrapping my arms around my body doing my best to warm myself up. I felt my body slowly curl up into a ball. One thing I knew was that this coldness wasn't coming from the air around me. It was coming from inside of me. It's my truth.

CHAPTER 18

"Please tell me this is the last one!" I begged, stepping from behind the divider in the hundredth dress. This one was long, light red, with flowers going up the skirt. It was tight at the top and flowed at the bottom. It would be impressive if I wasn't already exhausted. I'd been stuck trying on a dress, stepping out in front of Grace, doing a twirl, standing in front of the mirror so the dressmaker could point out the different aspects of the dress —like a dress wasn't just a dress—and then I went back behind the divider to do it all over again because my face wasn't happy enough for them. I honestly didn't know what they wanted from me.

"You look amazing in every one." Grace said with a smile on her face as I stepped onto the platform in front of the three mirrors to give me all angles of the dress.

I didn't hate a single one of the dresses, but I wasn't in love with any of them either. There was no point. They were dresses I didn't care about for a party that I didn't want to impress people that I didn't know. Not a single part of that seemed like a good idea.

I pulled myself out of my head when I realized how silent the room had gotten. "We must try another one," Grace said, and I let out a deep breath, turning to look at her.

"I can't try on another."

Grace raised her brows at me. "Because your schedule is always so busy?"

I picked up the ends of the dress to help me step off the platform, making my way over to her. "Actually, I would like to discuss something with you."

"Hm?" Grace took a small drink of her tea as I joined her on the cream sofa.

"I know there's a lot I still need to know, and I thought maybe I could...dip my feet in the water. Maybe get a taste before I have to handle all of it at once."

Grace paused, sitting in her own silence. She never broke eye contact with me, but I still couldn't tell what she was thinking. If she thought it was a good idea or if she was trying to think of a nice way to tell me it was the stupidest idea she had ever heard. Then her mouth moved up into a smile. "I think that's an excellent idea!" She reached over, placing her hand on mine. "I have a long list of meetings I must get done tomorrow with the coronation fast approaching. You will join me and add in your own opinion on what to do next."

My teeth found the inside of my lip before I asked, "Have you talked with Cordelia?"

"Since her declaration of war? No. She's spent most of her time sleeping. Whatever she is feeling has been keeping her awake for who knows how long." Grace sighed, shaking her head. "Fear is a crazy thing."

"What do you mean?"

"Our emotions can do incredible things. It can drive you to do things others don't think is possible. If that emotion is terror or rage, imagine what that can make a person do."

Grace paused only for a moment, her gaze staring down at the ground in front of her. "I believe that's what drove Anna to do what she did. There's no excuse for it, but I do believe she was suffering as much as a person could."

I swallowed hard, struggling to find the right words.

Grace shook her head, looking up at me with a forced smile. "But onto more positive outcomes. I will have Abbey bring you a schedule for tomorrow." Grace reached over, patting her hand against my arm. "Now, let's see what the next dress looks like."

I pressed my lips together, trying my best to ignore every protest in my body as I stood up and dragged myself back behind the divider. All of this was nice, but it could be all for nothing. The truth of reality was that after I was done, I didn't know what was going to happen. I knew how people would take what I was planning to do, and that was something I wouldn't be able to control. I could be forced out of the castle, I could have to give up my birth right, or…I didn't even want to think about what else.

INSTEAD OF TRYING to take a nap after trying on all of those dresses, I went up to my studio. Somewhere quiet. Quiet where I could give Lady Ophelia's journal another look. I needed to make sure I was prepared for anything. It was the only way to avoid any surprises. The journal was filled with different spells. Normally, I would just ignore them. There was only one spell I wanted, so the rest didn't really matter. Until I went a couple of pages too far. That spell was something new. It was just the intense feeling that it gave me. It was the way that reading it was like breathing fresh cold air. Air that felt like it was covering you in a cooling blanket. As if it was going to keep you safe.

Before, I would stay awake all night out of fear. I was too

scared of what I was going to see every single time I closed my eyes. This time it was different. I wasn't running from anything, I was chasing something. I was reaching out to take the things that were taken from me.

Just by closing my eyes and finally trusting the storm inside of me, I was able to change my bedroom into a different reality. A reality where I could see both of my parents. Crystal diamonds hung from the ceiling in the empty ballroom. People were going to be there any minute and we all knew it. Grace was in her element, looking at all the preparations that went into the party. I was something completely opposite. There was a knot in my stomach that made my hands shake and my body temperature rise. "Come," I heard Lucius's voice. I could barely recognize it by now, but a smile still spread across my face. When I looked at him, I didn't see the body lying in the ground surrounded by nothing but glass. I didn't see another life taken early by Anna's destruction. He held his hand out towards me. "I heard I'm an excellent teacher." I took his hand, letting him lead me into a dance. I stepped on his feet five times, and he still kept a smile on his face.

Eventually the reality changed. Not in a way that frightened me. Not in a way that sent panic or fear through me. A reality where I was with Kit. Sometimes they were simple. I would be walking outside, and he would come out of nowhere, taking me in his arms. Or he would be hunting, and I found myself running towards him to greet him. There was no fear or worry when he would walk away that he would never come back. He said he loved me every single time, but I never said it back. I could never get the words to leave my mouth. He didn't notice. He never even seemed phased. Then he would whisper in my ear, "I can see the love in your eyes."

This consumed me. When I came out, there was this new

sense of peace inside of me. My body felt as if it was floating on a cloud with nothing but warmth. Every worry or caution I had disappeared. It was a feeling I couldn't get enough of. I wanted more. I wanted to stay in those realities until they could last forever.

The first time only lasted an hour, then I found a tea to make it last longer; the more tea, the longer the time. I felt like I was drowning, but I was excited to feel it. I was excited to let the water take me over and take all the air out of my lungs. I wasn't reaching for death. I was reaching for peace. I woke up gasping with a joy inside of me I couldn't recognize. It made my mission that much stronger. I wanted so much more. I wanted the feeling all day. I knew I couldn't, but I wanted it.

Sadly, that seemed to vanish the second there was a knock on the door telling me it was time to meet Grace. It had been hours, almost an entire day, but it felt different. Like I lived weeks of a dream just to be thrown into a nightmareWhen Grace said she had a day filled with meetings she wasn't kidding. She woke me up before the sun even decided it was time to wake up. She felt the need to prepare me by explaining every step to the meeting I was going to take part in.

1) Meeting with the people

I knew I could handle the people. They just wanted to be heard and after years of feeling as if they didn't matter, I would give them that. I understood Grace and Lucius suffered the grief of losing their one and only child, but they stopped living. They forgot all the people they promised to take care of. They forgot everyone that was looking at them and waiting for them to step into the roles they promised to uphold. Honestly, the only scary part about this was having to sit on the king's throne. Grace said that it would be mine in such little time, it was time that I got used to it. I tried, but

I couldn't stop myself from shifting in my seat. I didn't want them to know how uncomfortable I was, but I could feel Grace glancing over at me. I just prayed she wouldn't say anything.

2) Meeting with the treasury

I knew I could handle the treasury meeting. Doan liked me. I think a little more than I liked him. Plus, it wasn't in the throne room which was a major plus for me. I just had to sit at the end of a table where Doan would lay out the budget: what we spent, what we gained, what we needed, who we owed, where we needed to be before the new year cycle. He talked for at least two hours. Grace poked my rib, not so gently, when she saw me starting to slouch. It was going to be more, but Grace ended the meeting because we had others to go to. Grace expected me to listen, then suggest a plan Doan would create, turn in to me, and I would eventually approve. The only danger in that meeting was me throwing myself out the window.

3) Meeting with the military

The military was a different story. It was held in the war room and we all just stood around the table. The air was thick with tension even without a fight surrounding us. It all happened in twenty minutes. My feet didn't even have a chance to hurt in the heeled shoes Grace forced me into. They labeled the kingdoms they thought were threats, said what they had planned if any of the kingdoms made a move, and then it ended. If there was 'a war in the air,' Cordelia was the only one who smelled it, and, as Grace told me, she was still resting. I didn't have to say anything, and after the headache listening to Doan gave me, I was more than grateful.

4) Meeting with religious officials

The last one was the only one that put an aching knot in my stomach. I was back in the throne room, but it wasn't the seat that was bothering me. Father Gregory decided to show up. Looking at his face only brought flashes of the last time we saw each other. I whipped around, thrusting my hand towards him, and a ball of power generating from my hand into him. He flew across the room, against the wall just to fall to the ground. I closed my hand, the color quickly leaving my face. Something about 'last minute changes.' I didn't care to listen. I could only hear the tiny whispers of destruction begging to be let free. From what I gathered, this was not a common meeting. It was just requested. They wanted to build a new church closer to the castle, where the one that had been destroyed used to be. Apparently, it was believed the land was cursed, but they believed with the right leader, Father Gregory, it would be restored. They all stopped their speech, and somehow, I was able to find my voice, "I am not opposed to the idea of a church. If it is something people wish to have, they shouldn't have to travel so long to do something they love. I must approve all plans every step of the way, and I will approve who will run the church." I could see Father Gregory's jaw clench, but no one else seemed to mind. No one else argued, and he kept his mouth shut. I will admit…the power was intoxicating.

CHAPTER 19

*E*verything was in place now. All that we had to do was wait for the red moon to rise. With that, everything I had ever hoped for would be possible. I would be able to save Kit from the mess behind the veil. The only monsters that he would have to fight would be those that he chose to fight. He would have a safe place to sleep without having to worry about someone trying to kill him. He would be able to have everything I could give him.

The problem with being left to wait was that the seconds felt like minutes and the minutes felt like hours. I had to find a way to keep myself from dwelling on the fact that I was left waiting, and hoping nothing else could get in my way. There weren't enough duties in the world that could make that sit well with me. Staying in my bedroom or going up to my studio wasn't helping either. One was filled with deafening silence and the other was too close to Anna. I didn't want to see her or talk to her until I was able to get rid of her. Once Kit was back, I would find a way to get rid of the door and her along with it.

So, instead of being in either of those rooms, I went to the seamstress room. Beatrice was there fixing everyday dresses that got snagged or needed the jewels to be fixed. She had more than one would think she would. "I always pictured rich people just throwing their dresses away when they get snagged," I said, from one of the tables I was sitting on with my feet dangling in the air.

Beatrice chuckled, the skirt of a yellow dress sitting in her lap as she sewed the bottom. "Some people do, but Raya has them taken, washed, and brought to her for extra fabric and gives the servants a tip for it."

"Why doesn't she just wash them and sell them or give them away? Seems like a waste to tear them apart."

"She tried that. Apparently, one of the noble daughters saw someone else in her dress and got so mad, demanding the dress back and the money paid for it. Taking the dresses apart and using the fabric saves a lot of hassle."

I watched Beatrice work with a sweet smile plastered on her face. She enjoyed this work. When I saw her this happy, all I could think about was how much she'd lost. She didn't talk much about her parents. All she had was her brother and now he was gone too. My stomach filled with guilt so fast that I couldn't stop it. "I'm sorry about everything that has happened because of me." The words seemed to come out of my mouth before I could think about stopping them.

Beatrice's whole body tensed before looking over at me. "Nothing that happened was because of you."

"How can you say that?"

"Because it is the truth!" Beatrice moved the dress to the side, standing up from her small stool to face me. "If you wouldn't have come here, I can tell you exactly what would have happened. Kit would have probably died in the dark forest, millions of people—hundreds of villages—would have been wiped out from the disease, no one would have realized what Anna was doing until it was too late, the war would have happened, but no one would have been able to stop her, the land around us would be shattered, and we would all be dead." She sighed, reaching over to place her hand over mine. "I know that moving on from Kit and taking on the responsibilities that once belonged to your father has been hard, but look at what you have gained. You now have a family and friends, you will be Queen in no time, and all the lives you have changed will have gone unmatched. You must focus on the positive. It's the only way to survive."

Positive…I could do that.

I was positive that I was going to get Kit back.

I was positive that I was going to get rid of Anna.

I was positive that I was going to kill Odes.

I was positive that I was going to fix all of this.

That was what I was positive about. Those were the things that I could guarantee. Those were the positives that I could focus on. Those were the positives that kept me going. Those were the positives that were going to make this all worth it. Everyone that I had lied to, everything that I would be risking, and the risk of using my power, the power raging inside of me, would all end up together in a sense of peace. That was what had to happen to make it all better.

After leaving Beatrice, I found Cordelia standing in the hall, staring out the window with a blank look on her face. Her blue hair was thrown all over the place, like it hadn't been brushed in days. She was wearing her blue dress, but the thin straps had fallen off her small shoulders. Not only had she clearly not been eating, but her skin was a sickly pale . "Glad to see you are out of your room," I spoke as I walked over to her.

Cordelia slowly looked over her shoulder at me. She

looked into my eyes for a second before looking back outside the window.

"How are you feeling?" I asked, watching her face very carefully. The only thing that changed was the single tear that ran down her cheek. "Cordelia?"

"No one else feels it." Her voice came out in a scared whisper. "They all think I'm mad. That something has clogged up my mind, but I know the truth. I know what is coming." Her eyes snapped towards me with a terror that made me jump slightly. "I know you have to feel it. I know you see what is happening. The line is being blurred between what is right and what is wrong, and when that happens only death can survive."

I held in a shaky breath, trying to keep my nerves from showing. "I think what you need is a sandwich, some warm tea, and a nap."

"I need someone to believe me."

I let out the shaky breath that I had been holding in. Her words struck a chord in me. I couldn't deny the truth was there—that there was a chance this could all go wrong. I would be blind to not see the risks in what I have been doing. Reckless? Maybe. Stupid? No. I stepped closer, placing my hand on her shoulder. Her skin was cold to my touch. "I believe you."

Her eyes glossed over with tears as she stared at me in disbelief. She had been told so many times she was wrong or crazy, she was probably starting to believe it. "You do?" Her voice came out weak and shallow. Like if she spoke too loudly the words wouldn't be real.

I just nodded before telling a servant to bring a sandwich and tea to her bedroom. Cordelia walked down the hall away from me, and I felt myself watching her until she turned the corner. I leaned against the wall, feeling my knees getting heavy from my reality. Maybe she was sensing everything that could go wrong. Maybe she was seeing the future. Maybe all of this could go wrong—

No, no, no, no, no!

I couldn't think like that. I needed to focus on something else. I needed to focus on everything that I could control. I knew I could do this. I knew I could fix this! This would not be for nothing! I would stop any war! I would stop anyone or anything that got in my way!

I just had to make sure that everything was in order. I was going to find Tasar and Alice and make a plan. We were going to make sure there was not even a moment of this plan left unaccounted for.

Tasar was in his office trying to read up on one of his studies, and Alice was in the garden bossing the gardeners around about where the flowers should go. Honestly, I think both the books and the gardeners were happy to have me pull them away.

"The red moon comes in just a couple of days," I said as I moved up the hidden stairwell with Tasar and Alice behind me. "I know there is still a lot of time, but things are going to be chaotic, and I'm not going to be able to do it alone. We are going to have to make sure the opening is as secure as possible. We don't want many creatures—" the words died in my throat as I stopped in front of the door. My eyes grew wide at the slight opening in front of me.

"Please tell me you left the door open," Tasar said from behind me, but he sounded like he was a million miles away.

The only thing that sounded close to me was the deafening silence of pure dread. The air around me got so cold I was barely able to move as I slowly pushed the door open. Papers, tables, books, paints, and canvases were scattered all over the room. I finally found my speed when I saw the basket on the floor had fallen over and its contents scattered in front of it. I ran over to it, hoping I was just missing Lady

Ophelia's journal in the mess, but I knew the truth. There was no missing it. There was no finding it. "The journal is gone!" I shouted.

"Uh, Maisey." Alice's wavering voice got my attention.

I looked up to see her and Tasar staring at the misplaced door. Anna stood in the doorway. With the oversized dress and birds' nest of hair, she looked like a mess, but she still stood like someone in charge. I stood up, moving to stand in front of Anna. "Who was in here?"

Anna paused, tilting her head like she had something to think about. "Um…you?"

"DO NOT PLAY WITH ME!" I screamed. A scream I forgot I had inside of me. "Who was it?"

Anna started to laugh. Her laugh echoing from the walls. "You should have known you would be betrayed. People like us always are. The people who have the power and aren't afraid to use it."

"Maisey," I heard Tasar's voice and turned around to look at his pale face. "We need to check the tunnel."

"I'll stay up here," Alice suggested, and I quickly shook my head.

"No, I want you to go back to my room and see if, by some miracle, it's there," I explained, and she nodded before rushing out of the room with zero hesitation.

I walked over, sealing Anna back into her room before leaving with Tasar. We rushed through the castle, trying not to draw any attention, but also keeping our speed up. If we were drawing attention, there was no time to check. It all had to still be down there.

It had to be.

I didn't know what I would do if it wasn't.

The path down to the back stairwell took forever. Every hall just seemed to keep extending. Every staircase seemed to carry on forever until we made it down the brick wall.

Normally, it was closed. It was closed every time I came down. Now, it wasn't just open. It was gone. There was no border between the castle and the power hiding behind the wall. My feet felt like stones as I stepped onto the sand. I knew it was gone just by the weight of the room. There was no power, no voices, the door wasn't shut because there was nothing to protect. All that was here was stone. I felt cracks start to appear in my heart. It was like every part of my body weighed a hundred pounds as my knees struggled to hold me up. I was left gasping for air as hot streams fell down my cheeks. I felt myself slowly sink onto the ground, my whole body shaking. I felt Tasar's hand gently rest on my shoulder as I cried into the empty room.

CHAPTER 20

I had a plan. There was only one thing that I wanted, and I wasn't going to let anyone get in my way. I was careful who I told, I was careful to make sure no one saw me, I was careful to make a plan that was sure to go as smoothly as possible. This wasn't supposed to happen! If I didn't find the things before the red moon, I would never get him back. Who else would know about them?

"This can't be happening!" I yelled, pacing around the now-empty cave, my entire body shaking with utter terror. All the air around me was being sucked out, making it so hard to breathe. I didn't even know how I hadn't collapsed all over again.

"Did you tell anyone about this?" Tasar asked and I whipped around, glaring at him.

"No, I didn't! Why would I? Why would I risk everything I worked so hard for?!"

Tasar let out a deep breath, "We don't know who did this, but we do know what we have to do."

I just stared at him.

"We have to tell the Queen."

I quickly shook my head, dismissing it as fast as the words came out. "No, no, we can't! We don't need her!"

"Maisey, we just lost the items that are going to open the veil! We can't do this alone!" Tasar snapped, and I just shook my head. I didn't want to listen to him anymore. He walked over to me, putting his hands on my shoulders. He kept me from walking away from him, and his brown eyes stayed locked on me. "Imagine what will happen if we don't find it in time. We need all the help we can get."

I knew he was right. I didn't want him to be right, but I knew that he was. I could only imagine what she would say to me. I had been lying to her, I had been going behind her back, I had been putting everyone at risk... I looked up at him, tears welling my eyes with the reality in front of me. "What if she doesn't understand..."

"We have no other choice."

We had no idea who came in here. We had no idea where to find our stuff. He was right. There was no other choice. I looked at Tasar, slightly nodding. He stepped away from me, and I held my breath as I walked back upstairs. Every nerve I had was on fire. A splitting headache forming from all the thoughts raging, demanding to be noticed.

Grace was in the throne room going over some last-minute preparations. She looked up at me, and she must have seen the color had left my face because she only looked concerned. "Everyone out!" Grace commanded and I waited for the last person to leave, shutting the door behind them. "What is wrong?" Grace asked, quickly standing up and walking towards me.

I struggled to look her in the eyes, feeling the pit in my stomach become an abyss of fear. I tried to hold my hands together to hide the fact they were shaking so much. To have her know how much I failed. I didn't want to care so much. When I first got here, I never thought I would. "Maisey?"

"I...I did something." My voice cracked as I struggled to actually tell her everything I had done. Letting out a deep breath, I walked over to sit on the dais that held the two thrones. I put my face in my hands. "I couldn't...Anna wrecked so many lives doing what she did! People died that weren't supposed to! I just...I wanted to fix what was my fault!"

"What are you saying?"

I swallowed hard, knowing I had to look up at her. "I just wanted to bring Kit back..." my words trailed off like they weren't coming from me. "There was this voice—this shadow—his name is Odes...he runs the veil. The other side —where Kit is stuck. He's there because of how he died. He's there because of me. The only way I could make it right was by bringing him back. All I had to do was...a spell. I would do a spell and open it just long enough to get him out, close it back up, and never do it again, but today...everything I collected to create the spell has been taken."

Grace swallowed hard, her blue eyes never leaving mine. "What was taken?"

"A unicorn horn, a vial of blood, a sword of innocent souls, and the journal of Ophelia." I listed off the items I had memorized in my head. **The seals come from others with matching power of the first witch.** That can't be replicated! I felt myself quickly stand up.

"Where are you going?"

"I have a thought."

"What thought?"

I am not telling her about Anna. Not now...hopefully, not ever. "Just something that can help." I tried to walk away, and Grace grabbed my arm to stop me.

"You can't keep any more secrets."

"I'm going to fix this. We just have to find the stuff." I tried to walk away again, and Grace pulled my arm back.

"You risk our entire kingdom for one person!" she shouted at me. "That is not what a Queen does!"

"I'm not a queen!" I yelled back at her, ripping my arm out of her clutches, and made my way out of the room. I made my way back up to my studio to see Alice and Tasar inside talking. I shut the door behind me, walking over to show Anna's door with zero hesitation. Anna walked from her curtains, heading towards me with a smile on her face. "I went over that spell and the power needed for it. Not everyone can do it. I need to know who can."

Anna lifted her hand holding up a finger. "You." She added another. "You."

"Say 'you' again and I am going to punch you in the face," I threatened and she chuckled.

"I told you before that this isn't the only way to open the veil."

"Yet, the person took all of my things!"

"There is only one other way to break the curse with all the things you acquired and have the power needed."

"How?"

Anna paused, moving over to lean on the doorway. "It requires a sacrifice of the highest order. The heart of the feeble. Someone whose heart was broken so deeply, they vowed never to love again."

I looked back at Alice and Tasar as if they had any answer. Then Alice's words played through my head, "Beatrice was broken-hearted, never wanting to love again to the point it changed who she was."

My eyes went wide watching realization spread across Alice's face. "Beatrice," we said in unison when darkness came into the room.

"Looks like the red moon is coming. What a shame," Anna stated.

I turned on my heels, running as fast as I could out of the

room with Alice and Tasar not far behind me. We made it down the stairs when the castle started to shake. Large cracks appeared and paintings were thrown off the wall; people were screaming as they ran out of the castle. A storm was raging between the walls. I ran down the stairs, doing my best to hold onto walls and avoiding the cracks as the stairs started to crumble under me.

I made it into the room, slamming my way through the doorway to see Beatrice lying on the ground, the sword hovering over the center platform with blood dripping down its point. The screaming from the sword was so loud it shot pain through my entire body. I put my hands on my ears trying to stop the throbbing before my eardrums burst. I didn't know how I heard Alice scream, but I turned around to see her on the floor, bleeding out of her ears. Tasar was behind her trying to help her up, struggling to bypass his own pain. She was in more pain than us. This noise was killing her. "GET HER OUT!" I shouted the best I could, and Tasar hooked his arms under hers, pulling her out of the room. I turned Beatrice over, noticing the blood coming out of her ears. I felt her neck, finding a weak pulse. I tried to pull her out, but all the strength I had was fighting the screams.

I struggled to push myself up from sand and, running over to the stone, I took the hilt of the sword in my hands. I pulled it away from the power surrounding it only to have its force slam me across the room and into the stone walls before I dropped to the ground. "Maisey! Maisey!" I heard Tasar calling my name. His voice came out smaller than it should have as he stood over me. Tasar tried to talk to me, but all I could hear was the throbbing of my eardrums.

"We gotta get her out!" I yelled as he helped me get up off the ground. "Get her! Get her! She's still alive."

The pounding slowly slowed down, but the screaming

didn't stop. This time it was coming from upstairs. I have to stop the veil.

Tasar walked over to Beatrice, lifting her up in his arms. I picked up the sword again, running up the stairs. I ran down through the shattered castle of stone and glass. What was once beautiful was now covered in pain and ruin. I made it outside to see the red glow in the air, sending a pain through my chest. Inside of the large opening was another kingdom of rundown buildings, all holding a dull color, but I couldn't look at them because of what was running past them. Tall, short, small, large, big, lanky: monsters of all sizes came running towards the opening, hungry for the outside world. Guards stood doing their best to cut down anything that came through, but it wasn't enough.

'Stop them.' I heard a whisper calling to get my attention. I looked down at the sword in my hand, a red glow coming from my eyes. 'Stop them.'

I held the sword tighter in my hand, listening to its words and the chaos of magic raging in my stomach. I ran towards the opening, slicing, swinging, using my magic to throw them back through the gap. I ignored the screaming, the yelling, and the blood spattering against my royal outfit. I didn't have time to be squeamish, I didn't have time to worry about the creatures I cut down, I didn't have time to think about the pain in my ears or the aching in my body.

I didn't even notice I stepped through the opening of the veil until the world around me turned into a bitter cold. There was no chaos, but there was pain. Not physical pain, but a pain that was present in the air. I couldn't let myself slow down. I had to keep going. I have to close it.

I just needed a little more time. I just needed to stop them the best I could until... "Maisey!" A voice broke through the cold, sending a warmth through my entire body. I looked over to see Kit stab down another monster, making his way over to me.

"Kit!" It took everything I had not to run into his arms, but I didn't have time. "You have to get out!" I held onto the sword tighter until I was losing color in my knuckles.

"What are you doing?"

"I'm shutting the veil! You have to get through it!" A monster tried to run past me, and I swung the sword, cutting through the thin creature like butter. "Go! I can't wait any longer!"

Kit took a step closer to me, grasping my wrist and locking his brown eyes onto mine. "I'm not leaving without you!"

If my senses hadn't been dulled by the power raging in my hand, I would have burst into tears. "I'm not getting out!"

"Then neither am I!"

I looked over Kit's shoulder, seeing the dark storm coming straight for the opening. It was moving fast and brought the ripe smell of death along with it.

I was out of time.

I looked back at the opening, chanting the spell I read time and time again. Heat ran from my hands turning the sword red from the handle towards the tip. My body shook with power as I ran the tip along the opening, pulling the opening shut. The more I moved the sword, the more it felt like the air was slowly being pulled from my lungs. A sharp pain went through my chest, traveling through my entire body. I held on as tightly as I could until the world I had gotten used to started to vanish before me. The sword dropped from my hands as my knees gave out from under me. A strong, powerful roar came through the air, and two strong arms wrapped around me, pulling me up.

"We have to go!" Kit urged and I looked at the sword laying on the ground.

I tried to shout, "We need it! You have to grab it!" But my voice was gone. I could barely take in the air, words wouldn't fit. I was just stuck watching the sword laying in the sandy ground, its glimmer dulled the more distance came between us.

Kit and I were back, surrounded by the grayish trees towering over us almost like before. Only this was colder. The air was a bitter cold, but maybe that was just me. Maybe I was the cold, tainting everything around me. Kit only stopped moving when we came across a campsite that had clearly been used before. "Look at us, back where we started." I slightly smiled as Kit threw a rough, dark-green blanket over my shoulders.

Kit let out a deep breath, refusing to look at me. He just bent down to start a small fire in front of us. He didn't say anything to me unless it was demanding something.

"Why are you mad at me?" I asked, finally getting him to look at me.

"Why am I mad? You thought the dark forest was bad, this place is ten times worse. Everything wants to kill you, and now it's going to be even worse! You were safe! You could have stayed with your family, taken your birthright, started a family of your own, and you threw it all away! For nothing! I'm more than just mad at you!"

I shot to my feet, looking down at him. "I didn't do it for nothing! I did it for you! I was trying to save you!"

Kit stood up, towering over me. I had almost forgotten how tall he was. "I didn't ask you to!"

"You didn't have to! I watched you die! You stared into my eyes and took your last breath! Did you really think I was just going to be able to throw that away like it didn't happen! You died because of me!"

"I died because I made a choice!" Kit snapped. "I made a choice so that you would survive! I made a choice so you could have a life!"

A loud growl came through the air, and Kit's body tensed. He didn't move for a solid minute until we were surrounded by silence again.

"I am sorry for a lot of things," my voice came out quieter than I meant to. "But saving you isn't going to be one of them."

Kit let out a deep breath, his body deflating. "Maisey—"

His words were cut off by the cry of pain erupting from me. I held onto Kit to keep from falling to the ground. He quickly moved the blanket off my shoulder. "Where does it hurt?"

"My side!" I cried out in pain as Kit brushed the side of my dress, causing it to slide across my skin. Kit took his knife, cutting a small hole in the side of my dress, looking at my skin. "What is it?"

"We need to go," Kit said, looking back up at me. "We need to find somewhere safe."

"What is it?" I asked through the tears falling down my cheeks.

"You remember how I said everything is out to kill us? Well, they aren't wasting any time." Kit picked up everything he could fit in his bag. He took my hand, making sure I didn't fall behind as we moved through the woods. I tried to focus on anything but the pain, but that only left the chilling voice in the air.

'I'm coming for you.'

Lizzy Richmond has been in love with writing for as long as she can remember. It's a part of who she is and sharing her stories have been a dream she couldn't be happier in sharing her work with the world. She lives in Michigan where her family has lived all her life.

When she's not writing or reading, she's cooking meals for her family or playing with her loving dog Ollie.

www.ingramcontent.com/pod-product-compliance
Lightning Source LLC
Chambersburg PA
CBHW060454300726
48975CB00008B/2507